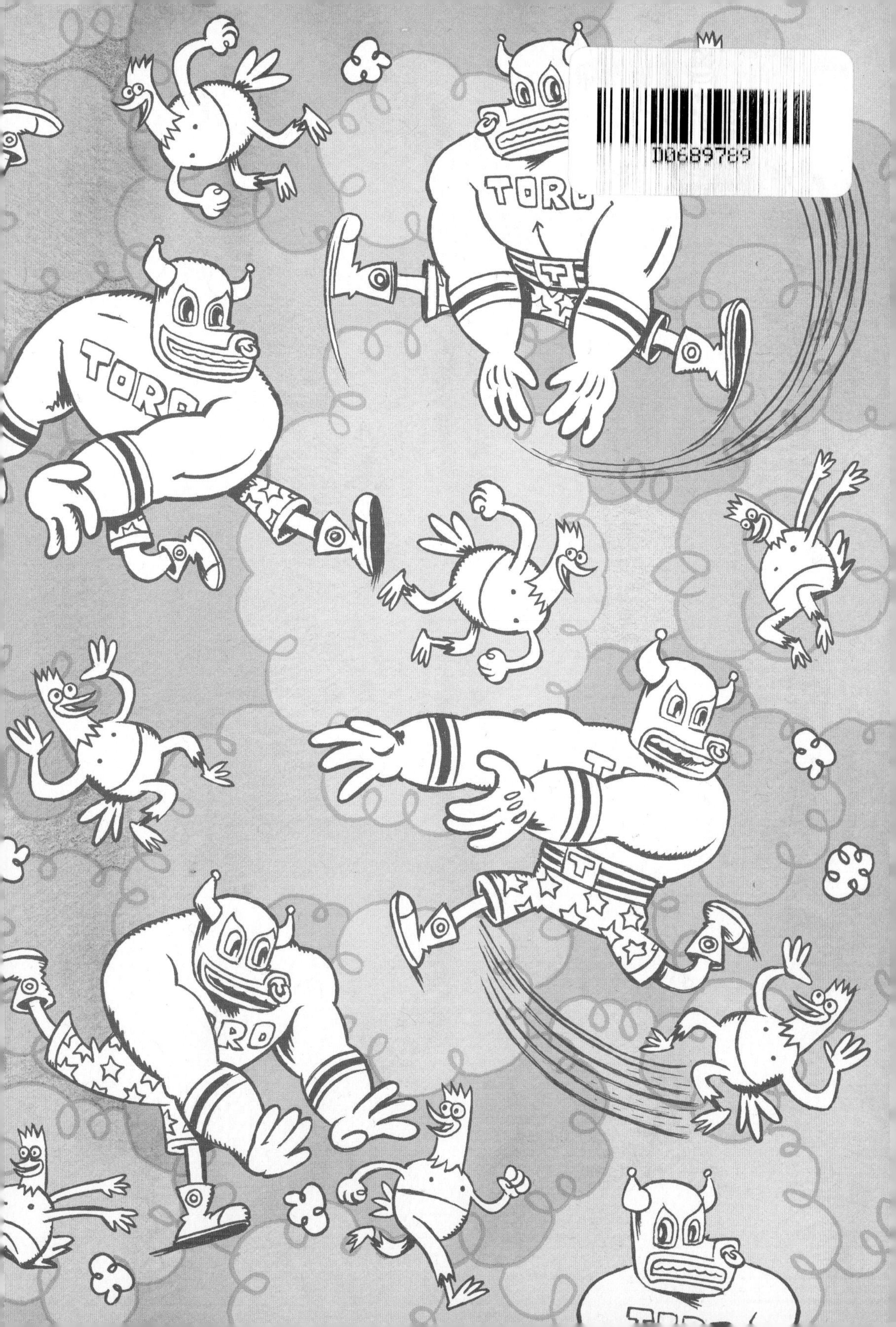
TORO
T
TORO
T
TORO

& Friends.

TAG TEAM

by Raúl the Third
colors by Elaine Bay

VERSIFY
HOUGHTON MIFFLIN HARCOURT
BOSTON   NEW YORK

Last night was exciting.
El Coliseo rattled and shook
with cheers and boos!

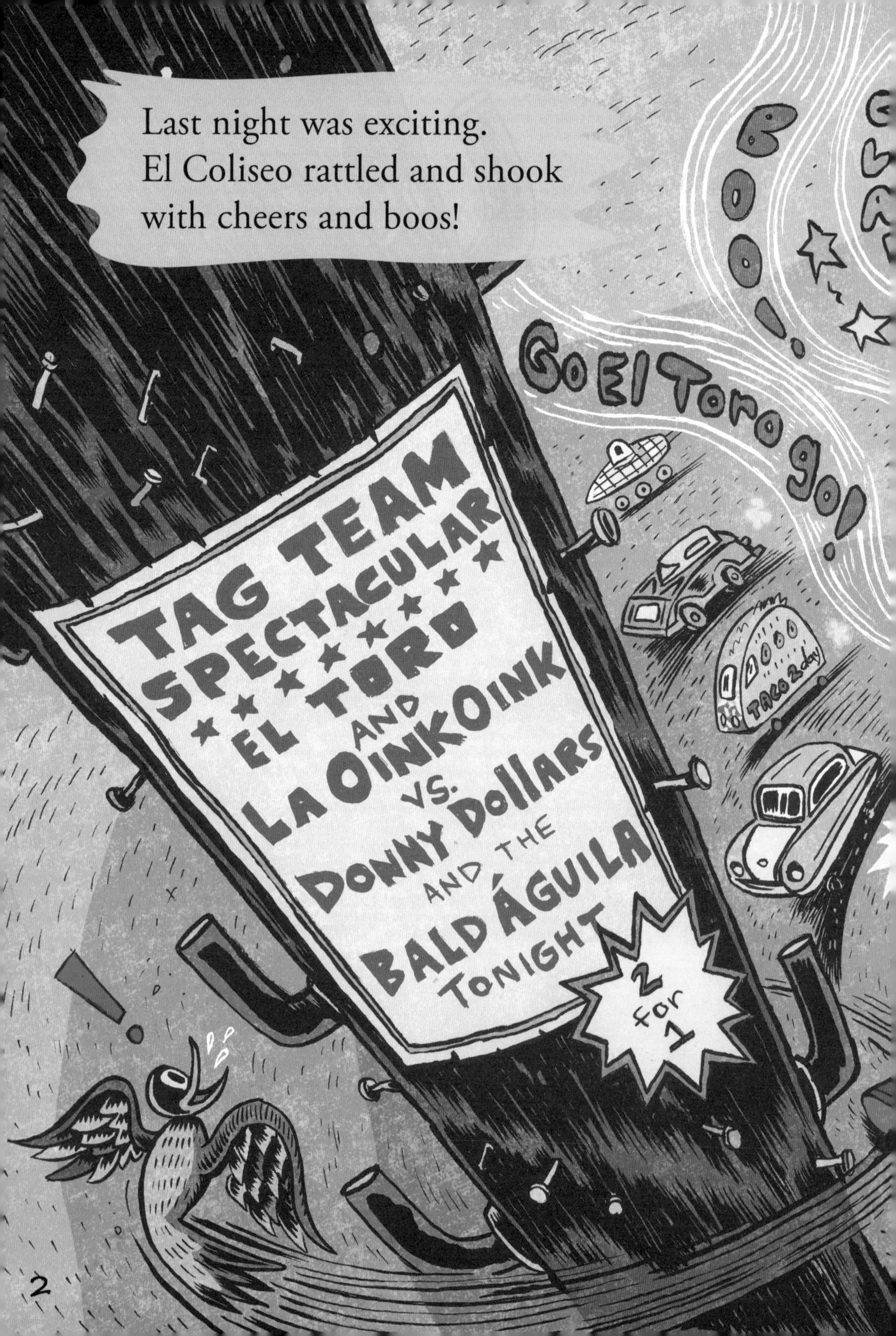
BOOO!
Go El Toro go!
TAG TEAM SPECTACULAR
EL TORO AND LA OINK OINK
VS.
DONNY DOLLARS AND THE BALD ÁGUILA
TONIGHT
2 for 1
TACO 2 day

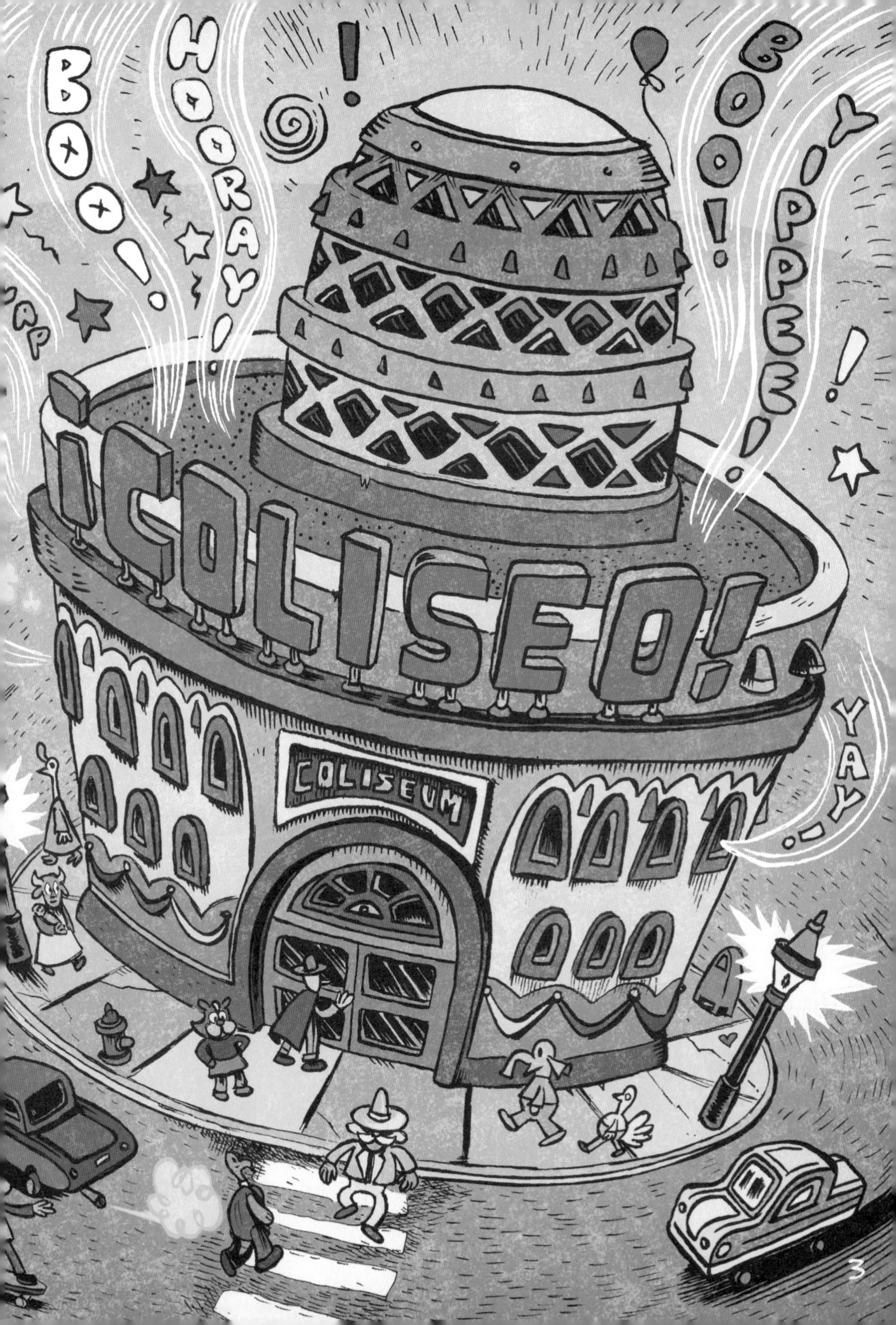
BOO!
HOORAY!
BOO!
YIPPEE!
¡COLISEO!
COLISEUM
YAY

El Toro and La Oink Oink battled Donny Dollars and the Bald Águila for the Tag Team Championship.

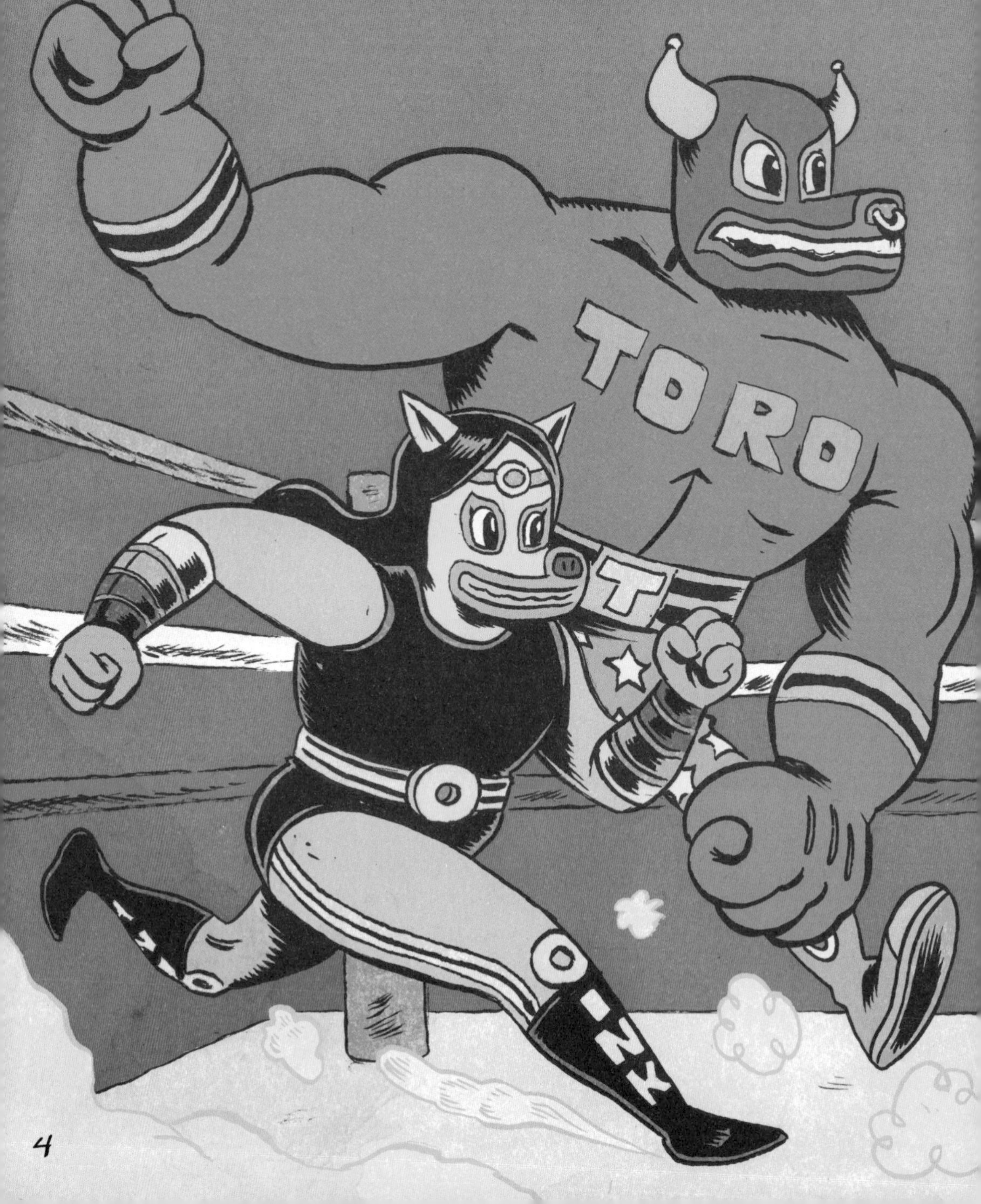
TORO
OINK

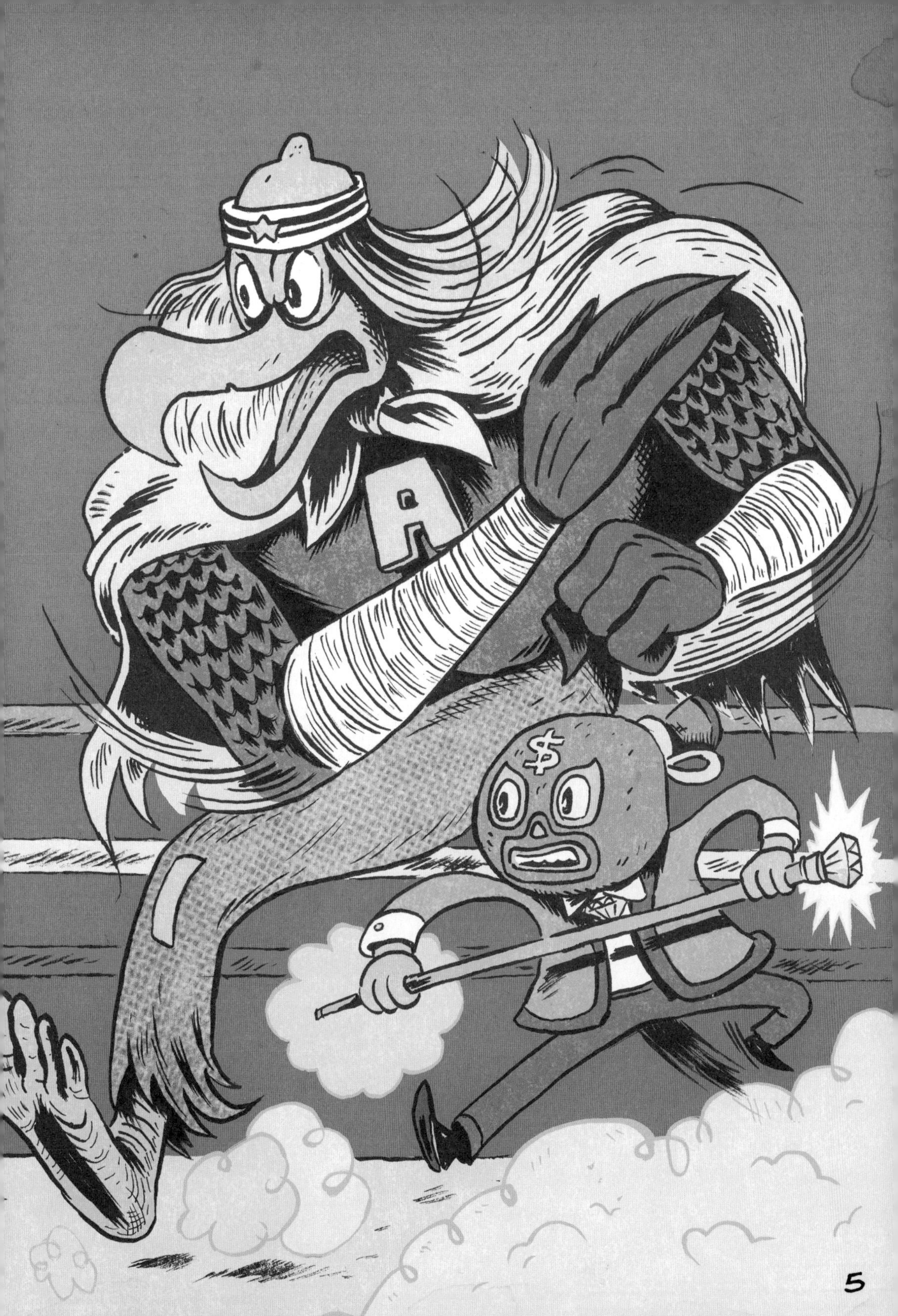

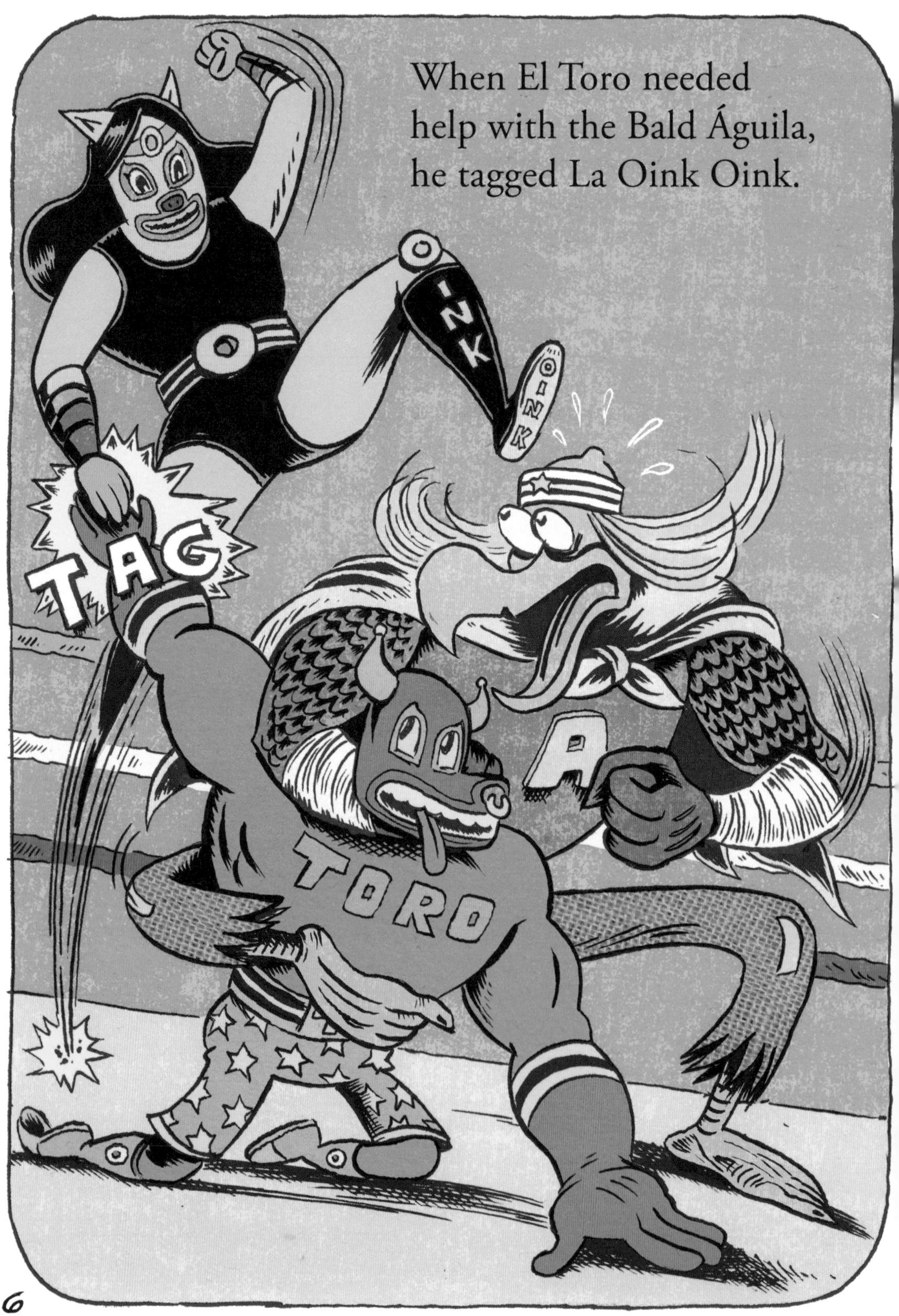
When El Toro needed
help with the Bald Águila,
he tagged La Oink Oink.
OINK
TAG
A
TORO

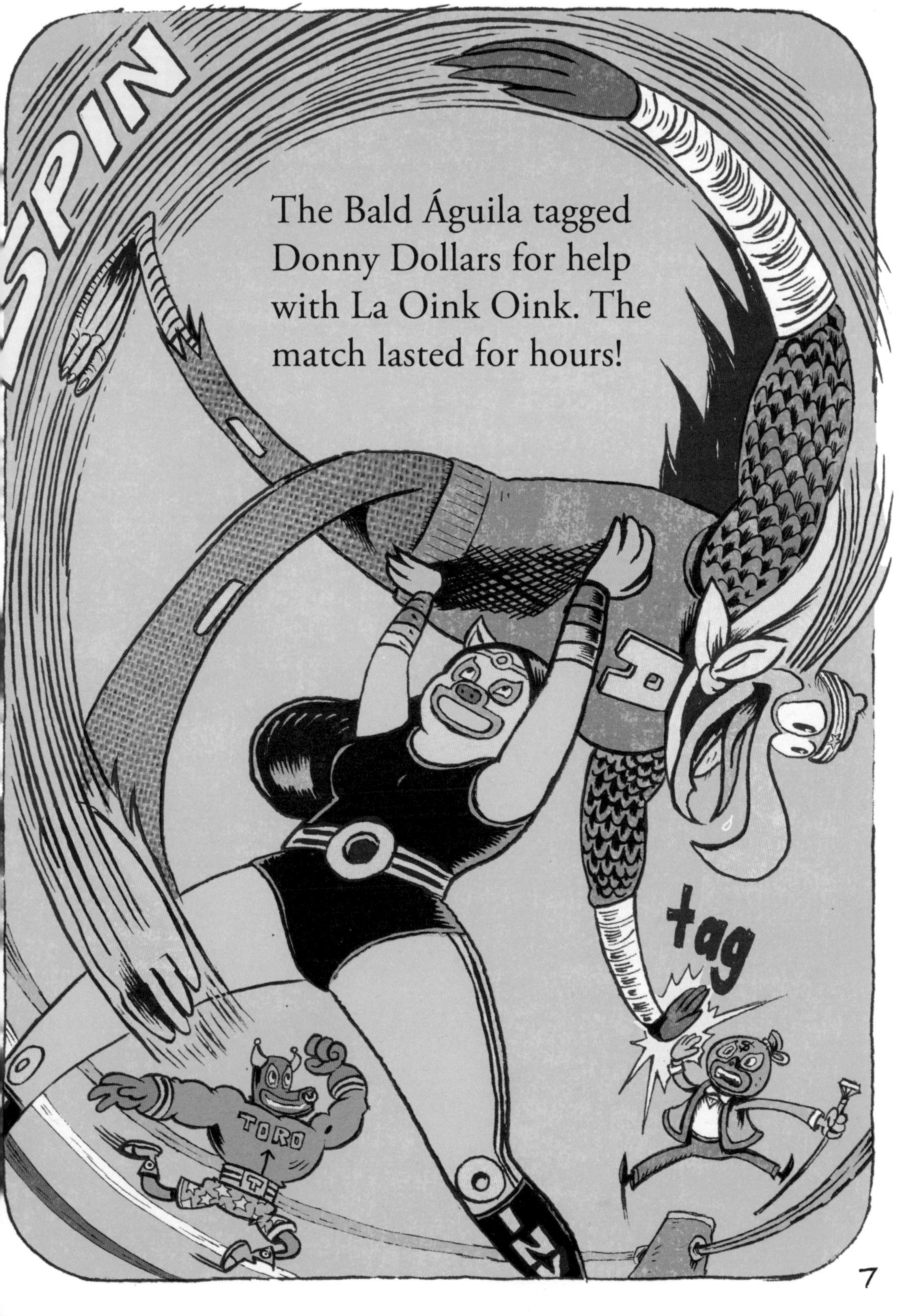
SPIN
tag
TORO

The Bald Águila tagged Donny Dollars for help with La Oink Oink. The match lasted for hours!

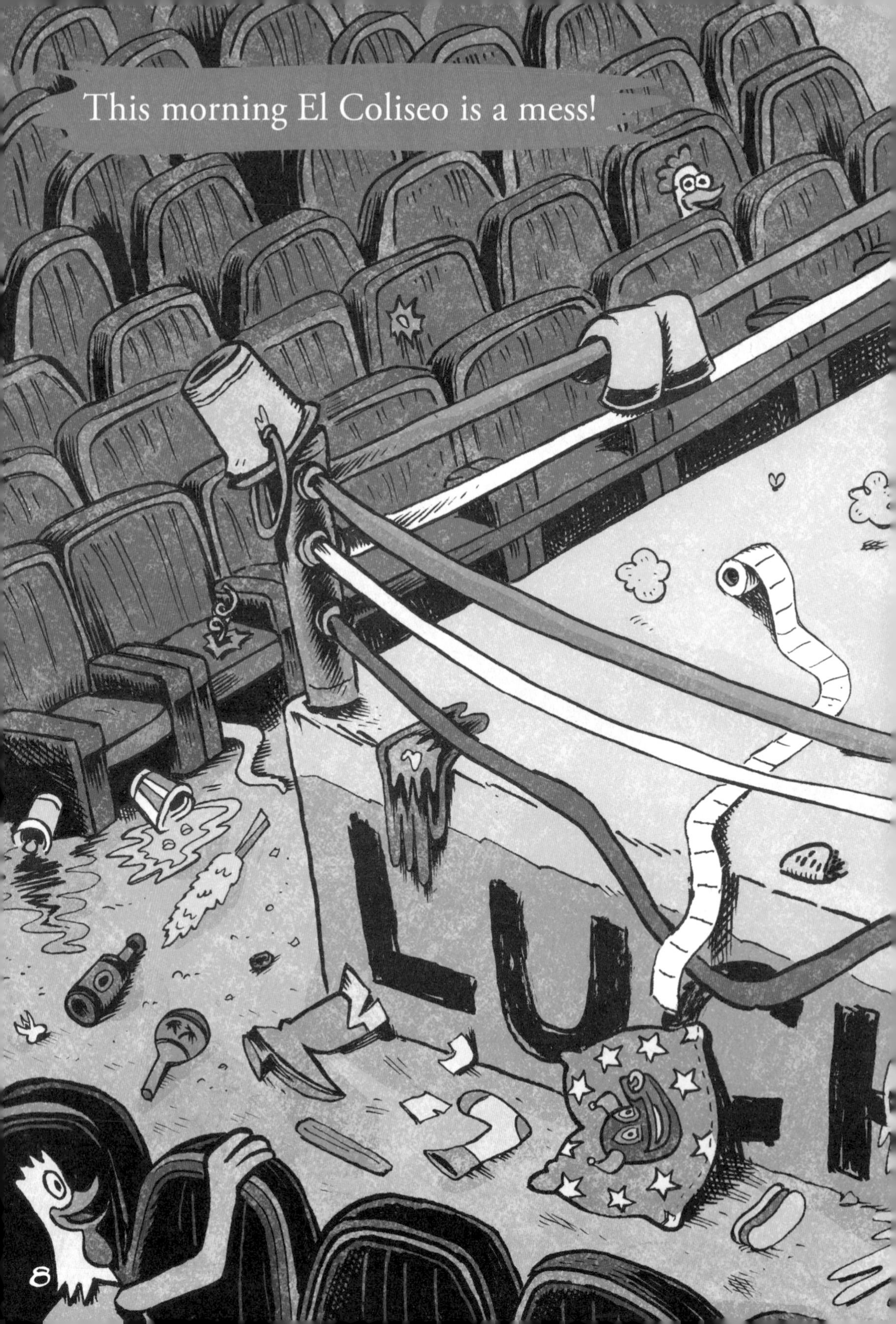
This morning El Coliseo is a mess!

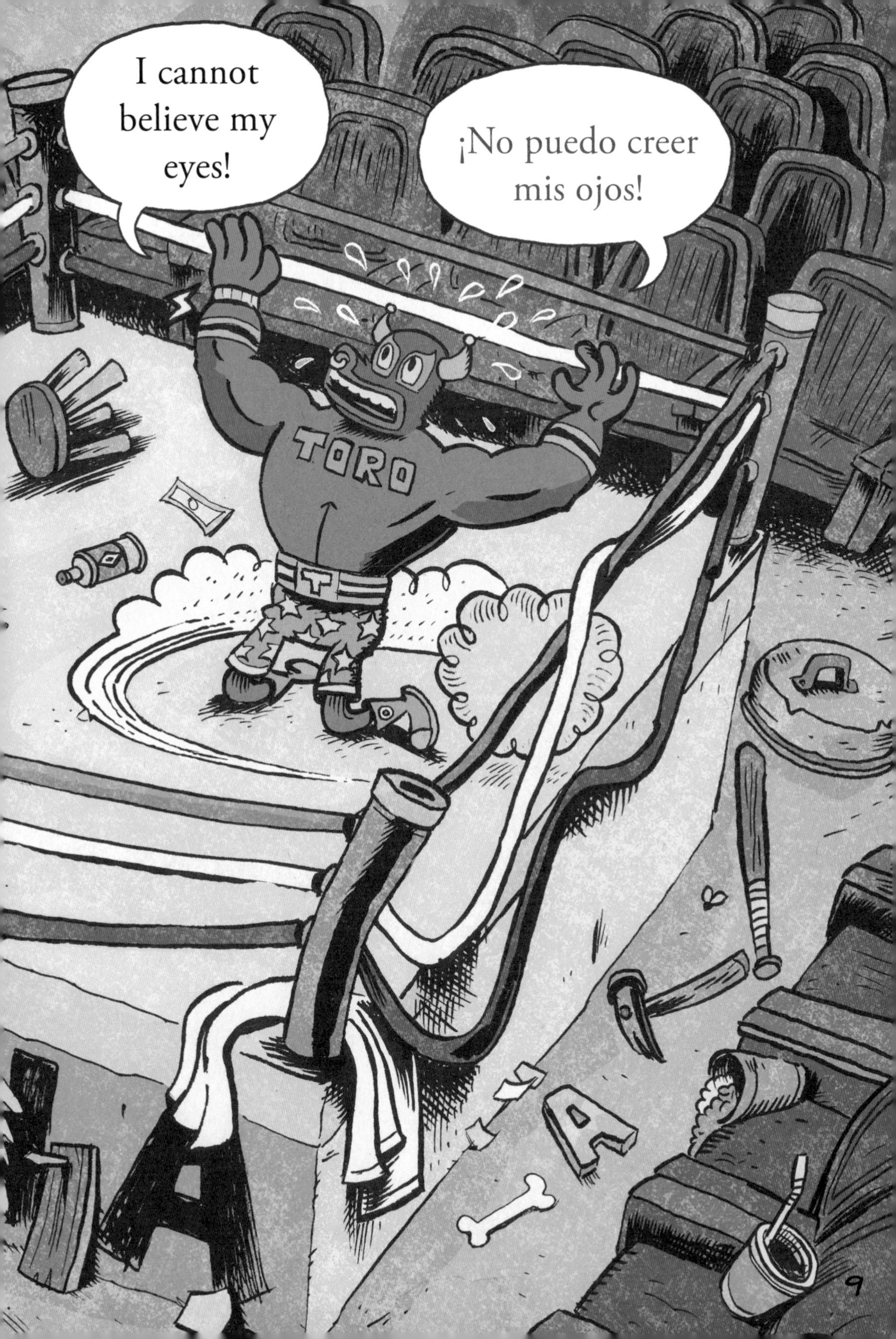
I cannot believe my eyes!
¡No puedo creer mis ojos!
TORO
T

Mal Burro and Peeky Pequeño are not coming in.

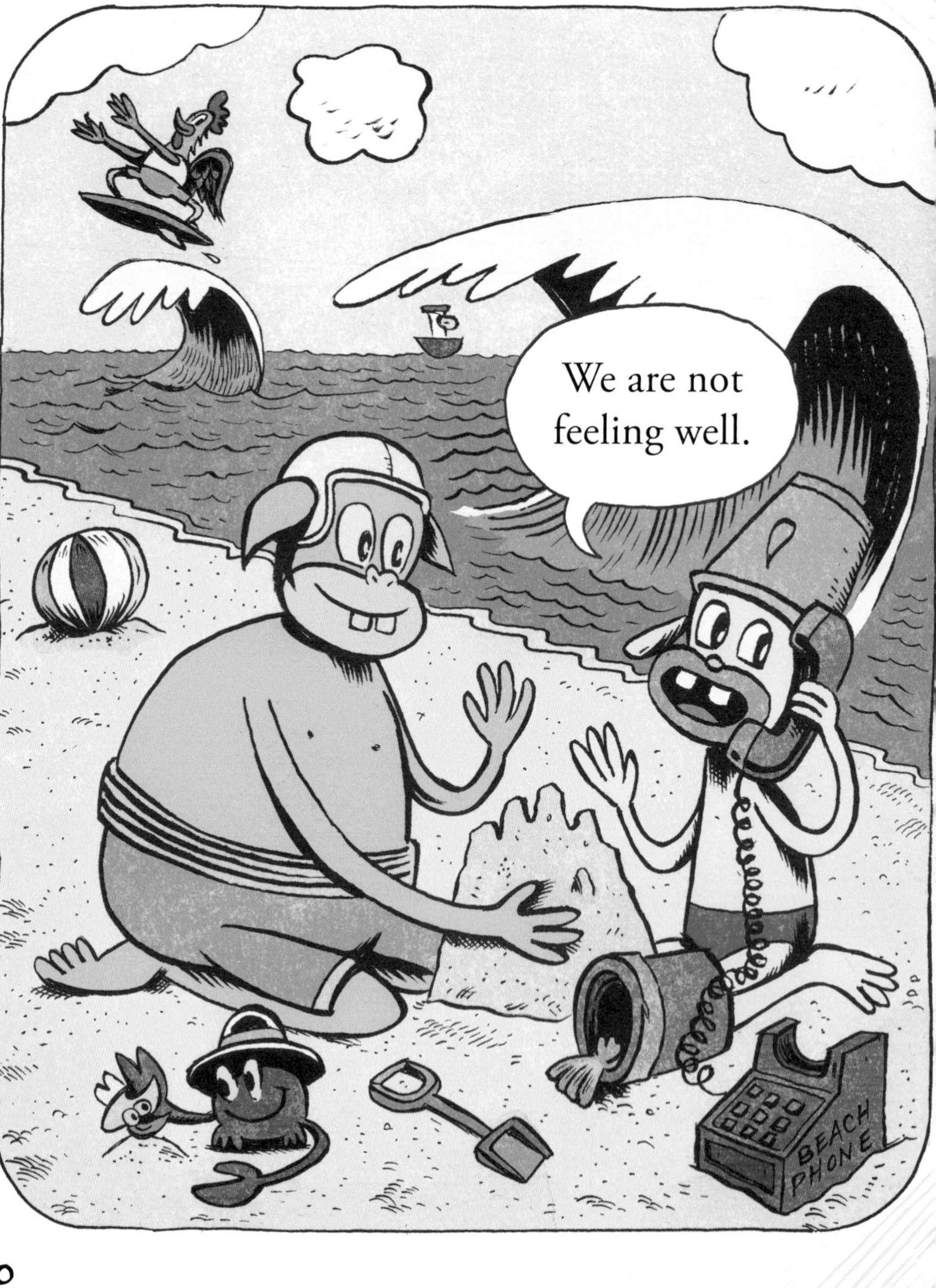
We are not feeling well.
BEACH PHONE

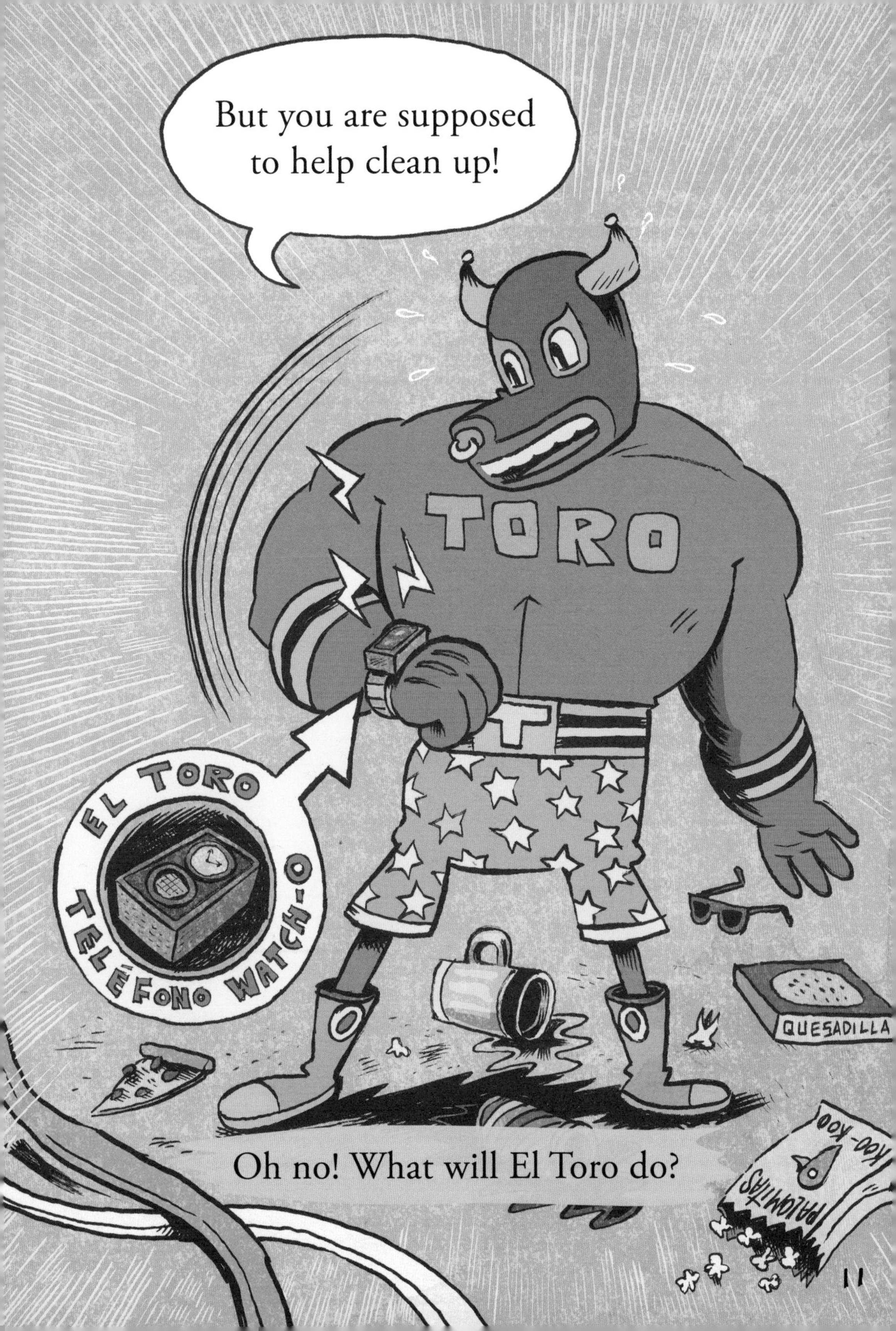
But you are supposed to help clean up!
TORO
EL TORO TELÉFONO WATCH-O
QUESADILLA
KOO-KOO
PALOMITAS
Oh no! What will El Toro do?

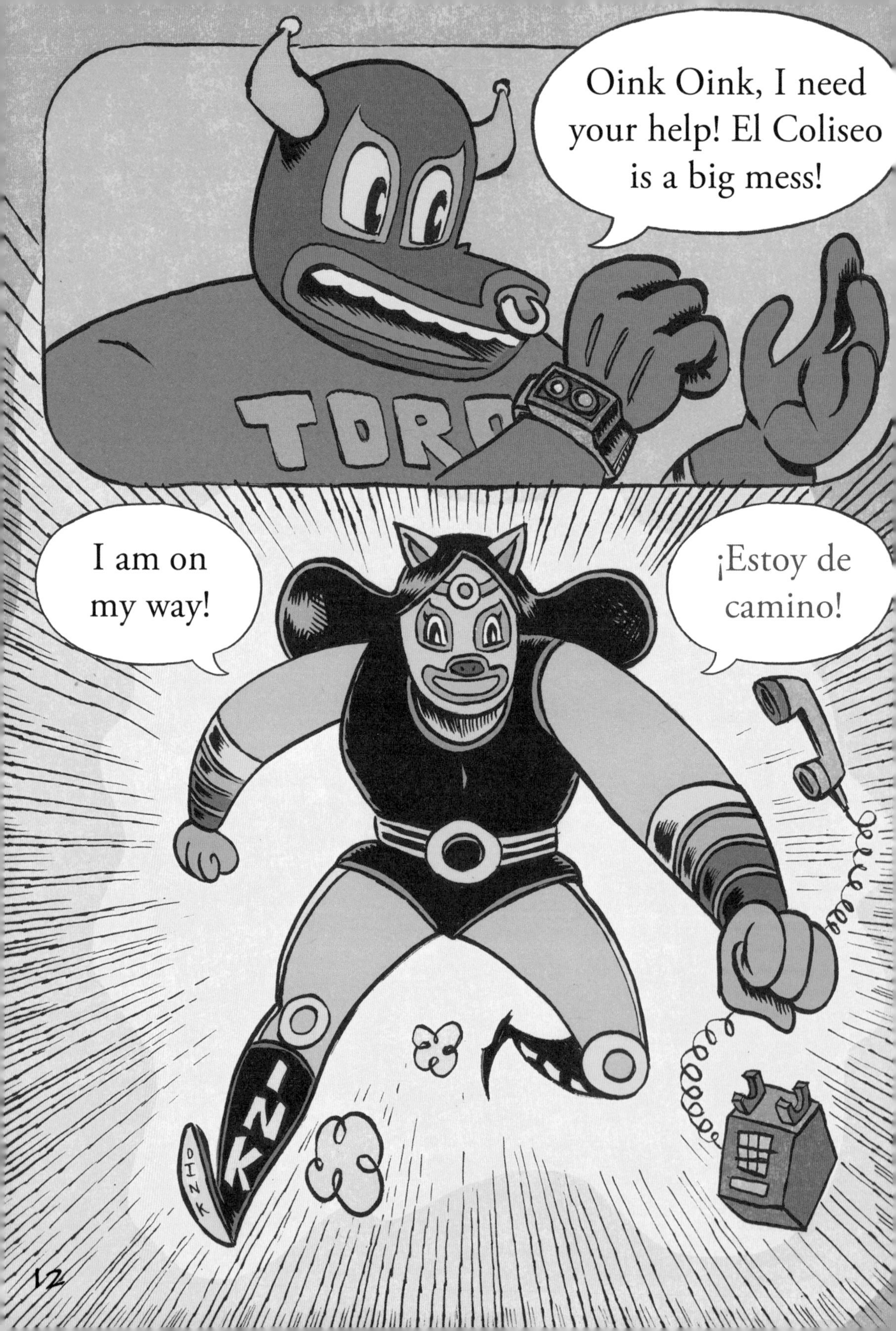
Oink Oink, I need your help! El Coliseo is a big mess!
I am on my way!
¡Estoy de camino!

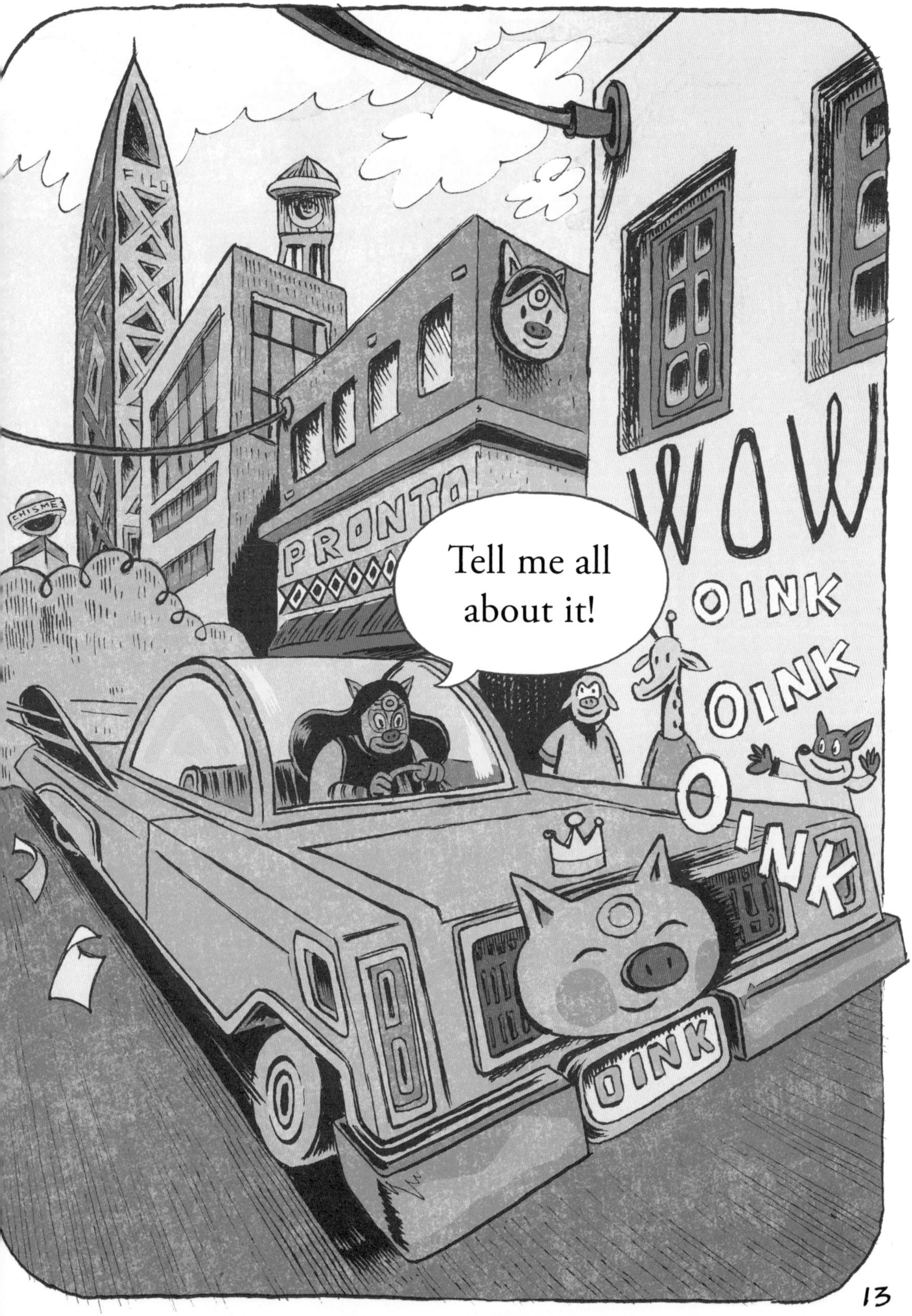
FILO
CHISME
PRONTO
WOW
OINK
OINK
Tell me all about it!
OINK
OINK

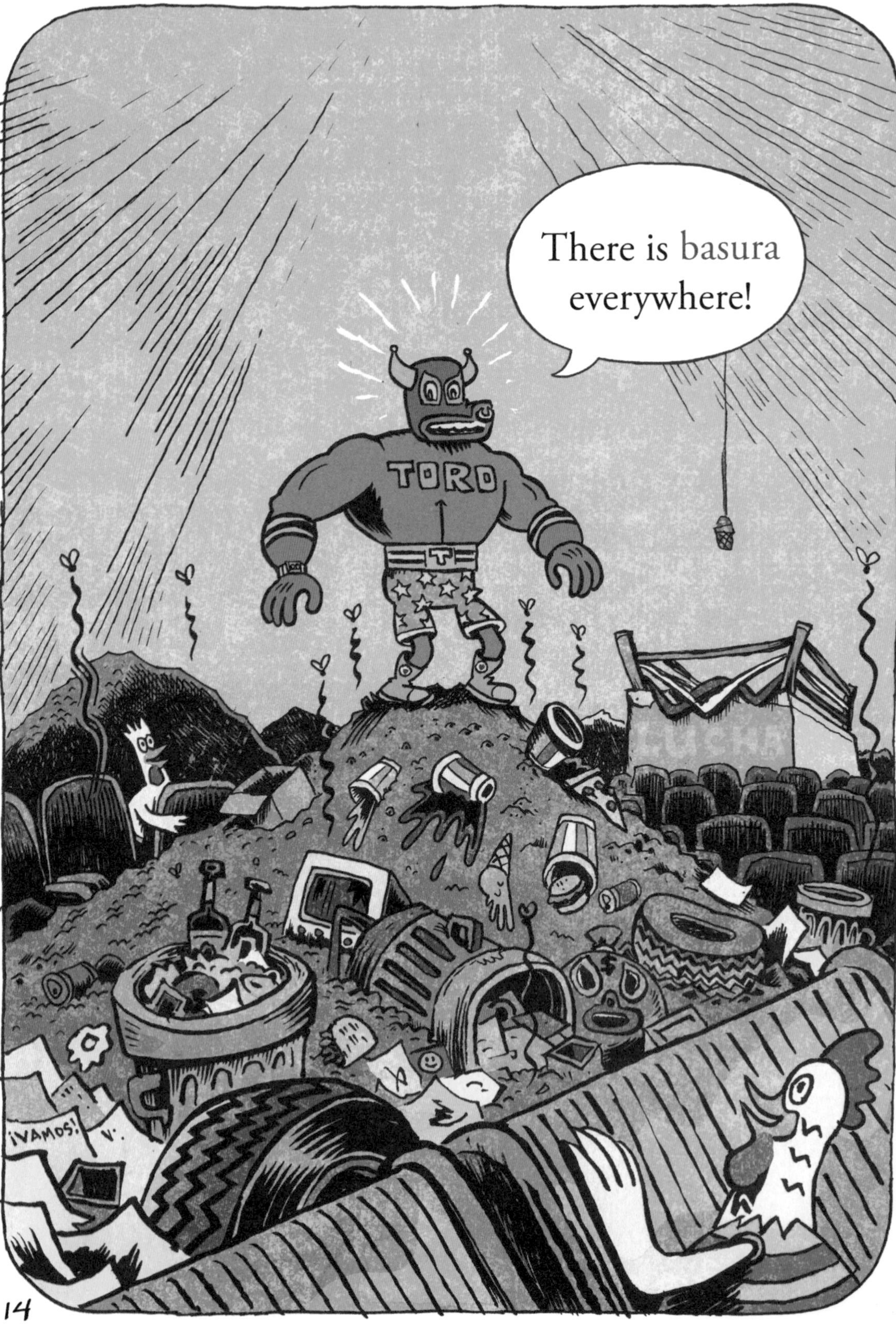
There is basura everywhere!
TORO
¡VAMOS!

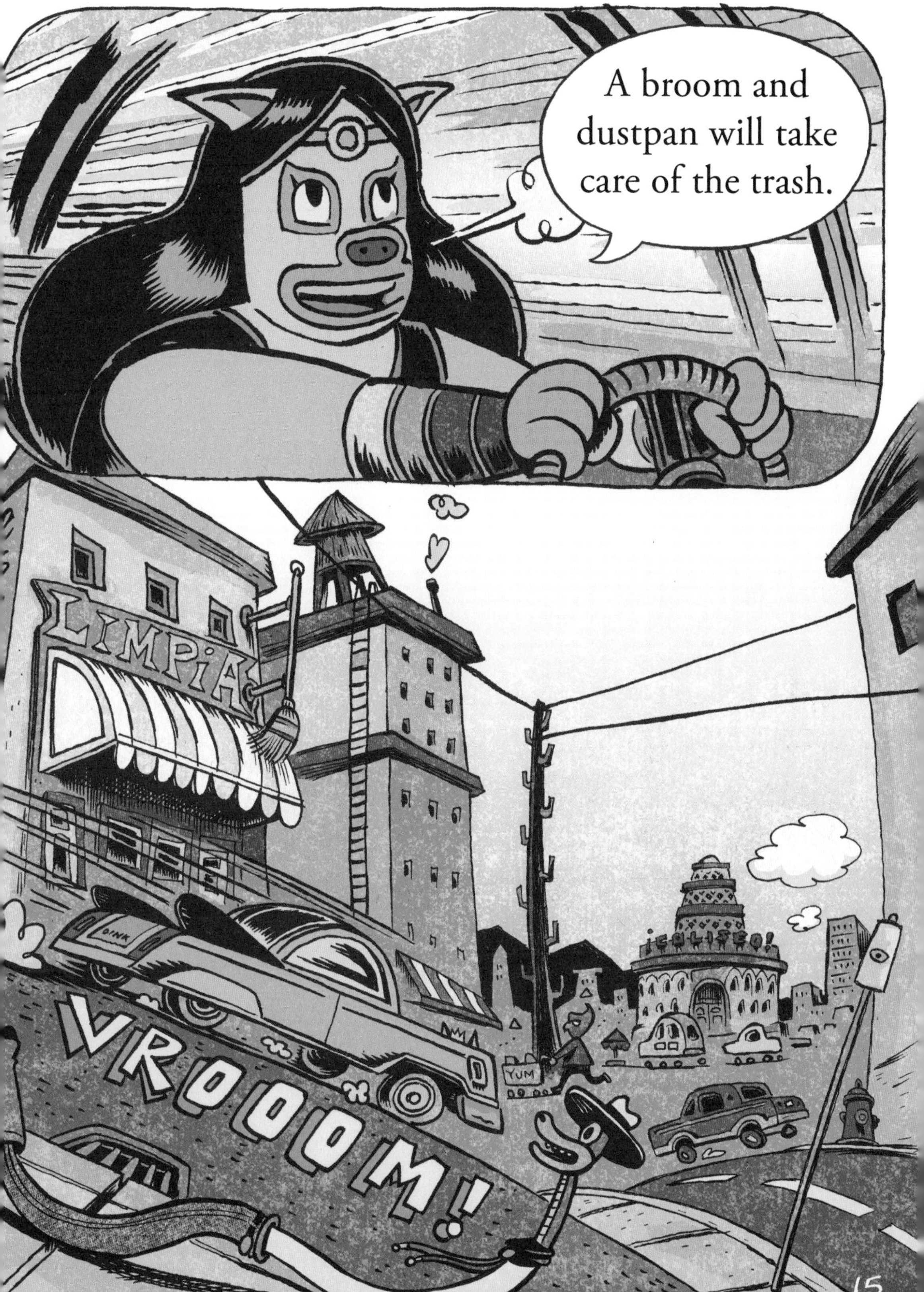
A broom and dustpan will take care of the trash.
LIMPIA
¡COLISEO!
YUM
VROOOOM!

The floors are sticky!

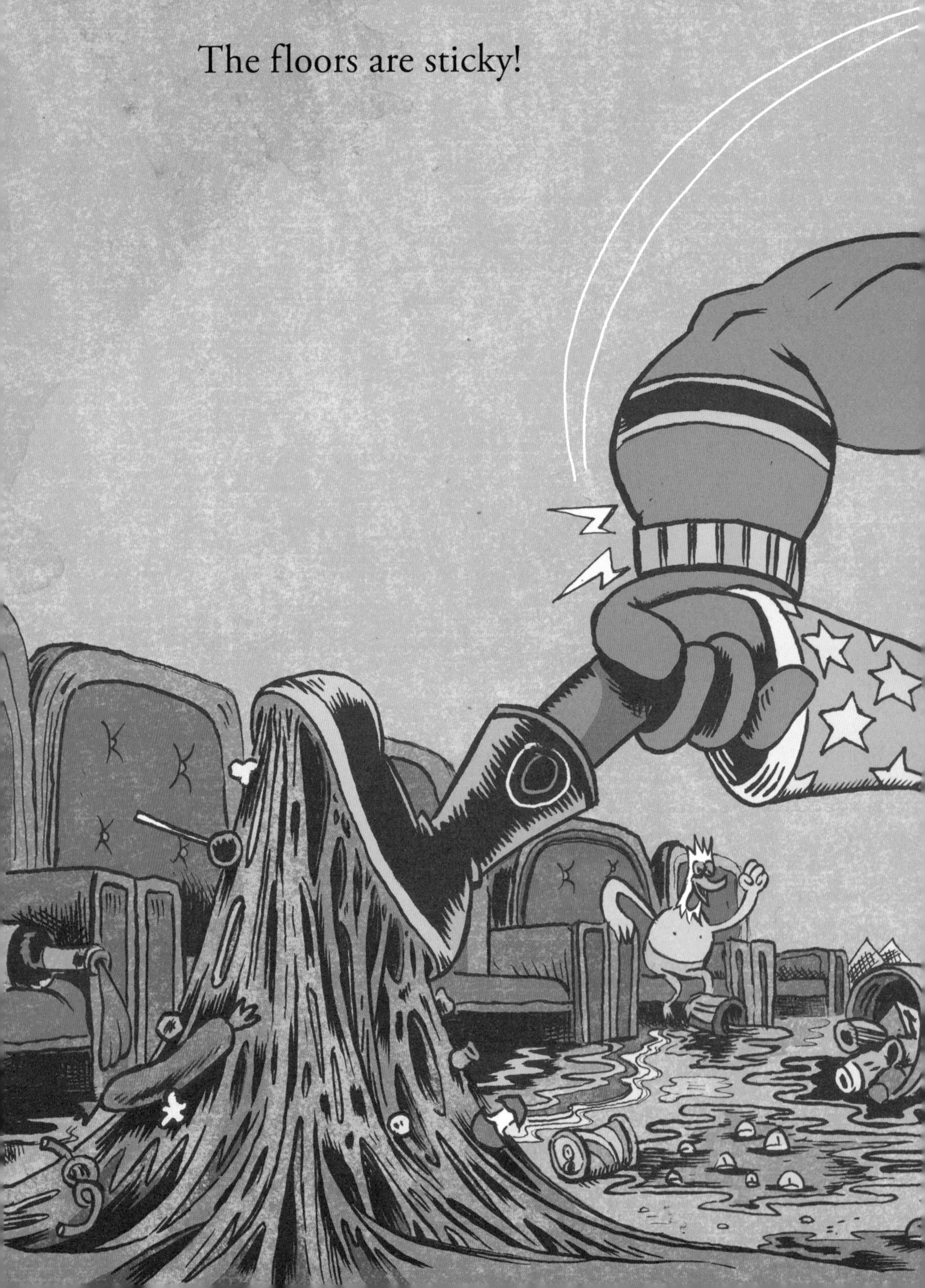

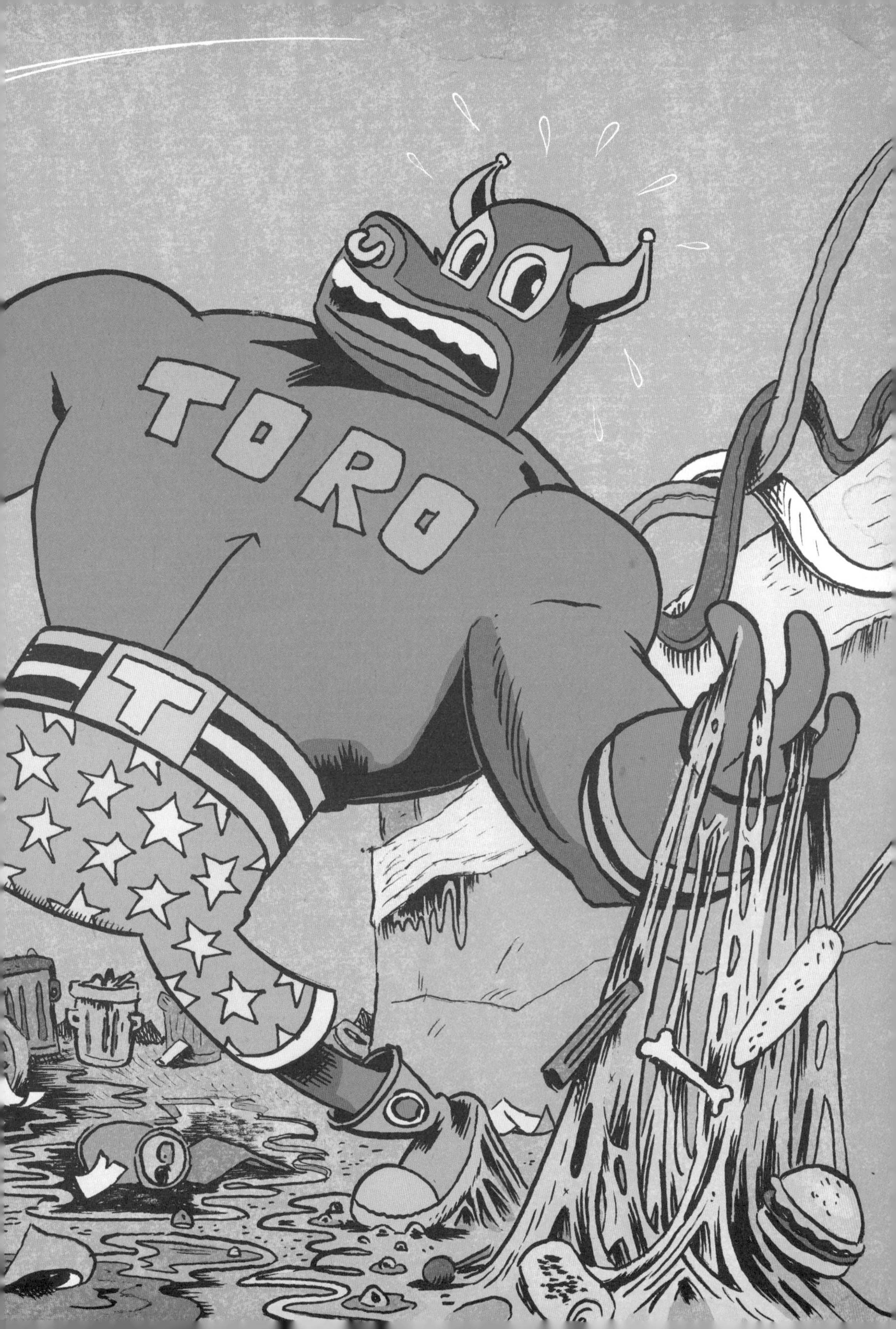
TORO
T

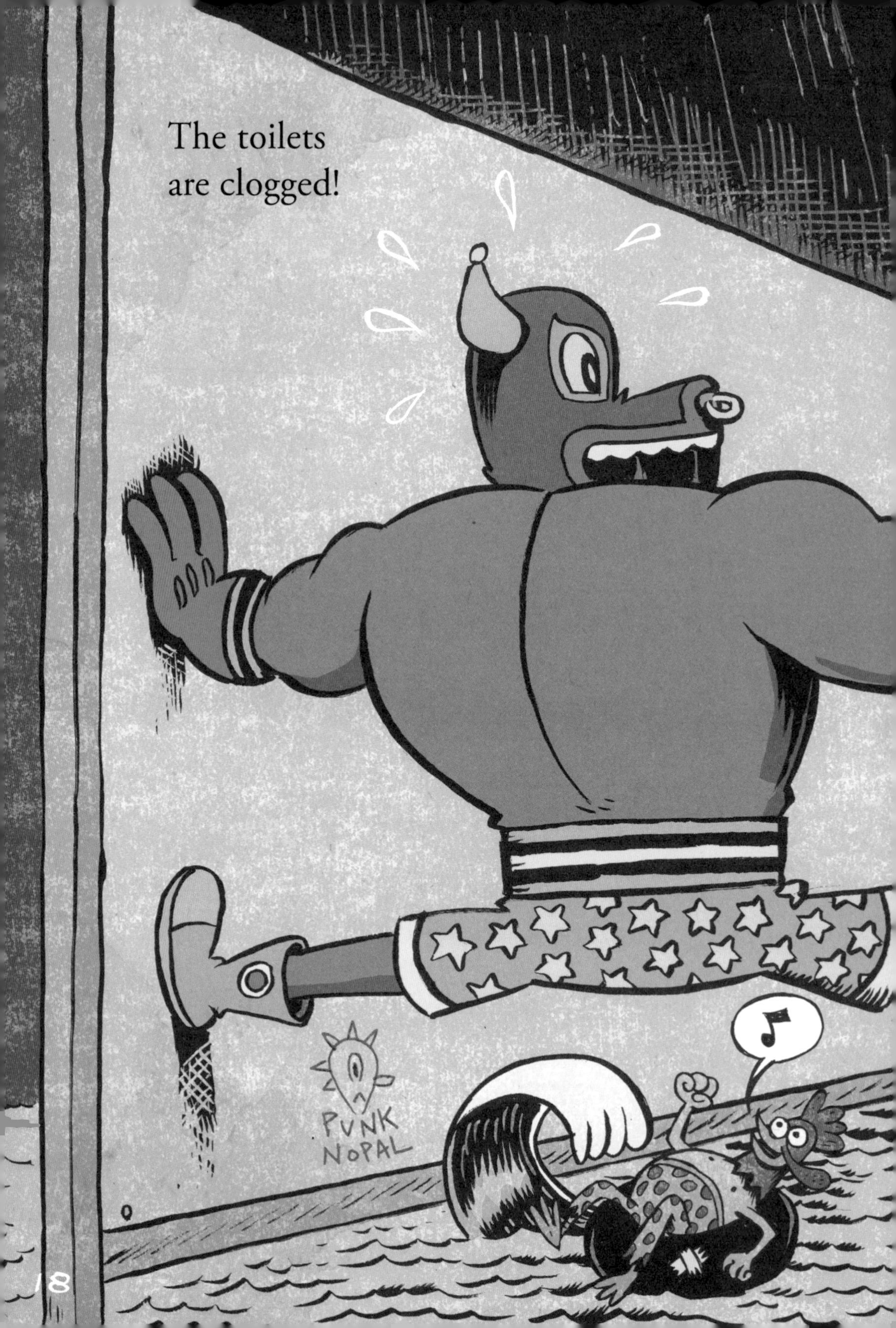
The toilets
are clogged!
PUNK
NOPAL

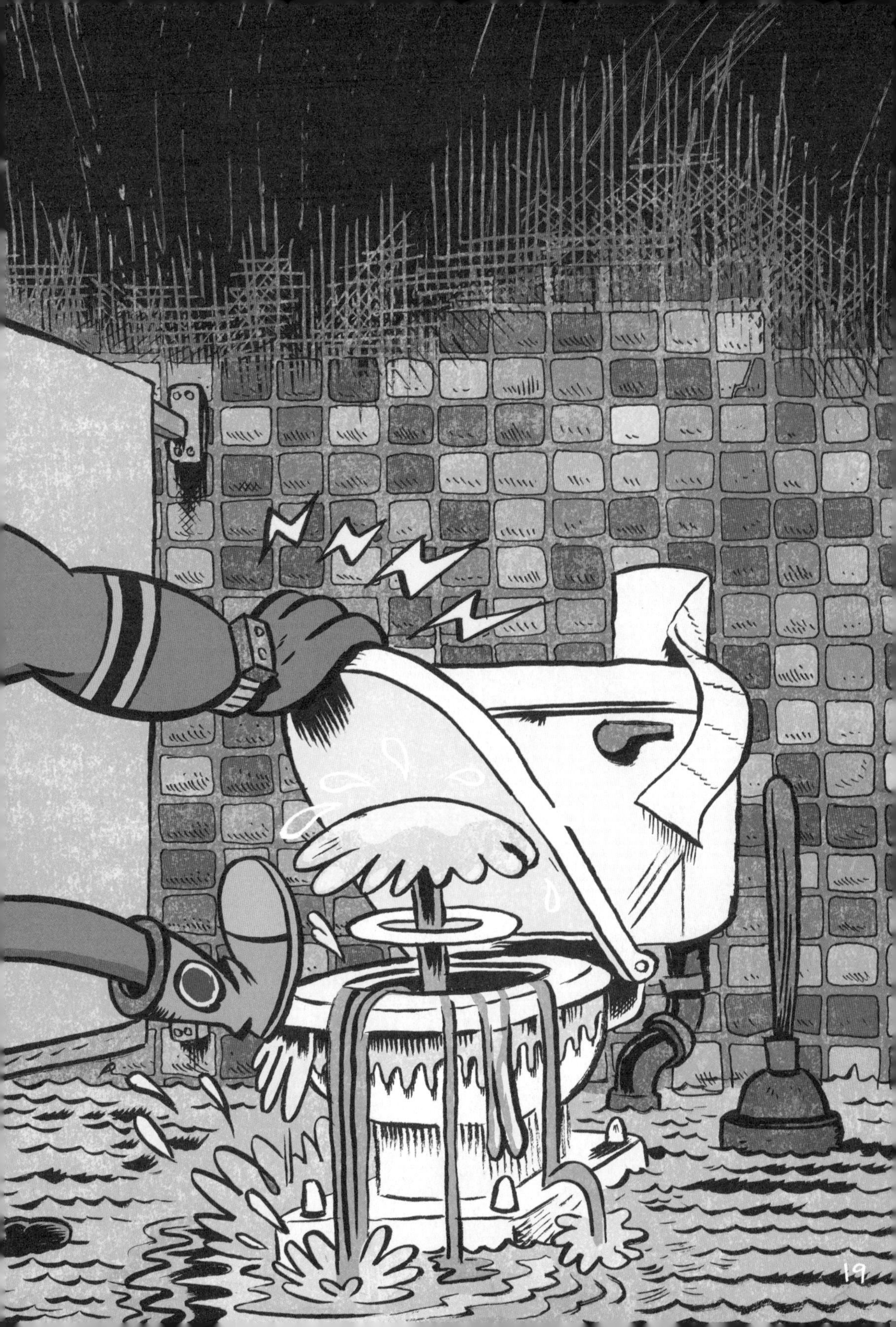

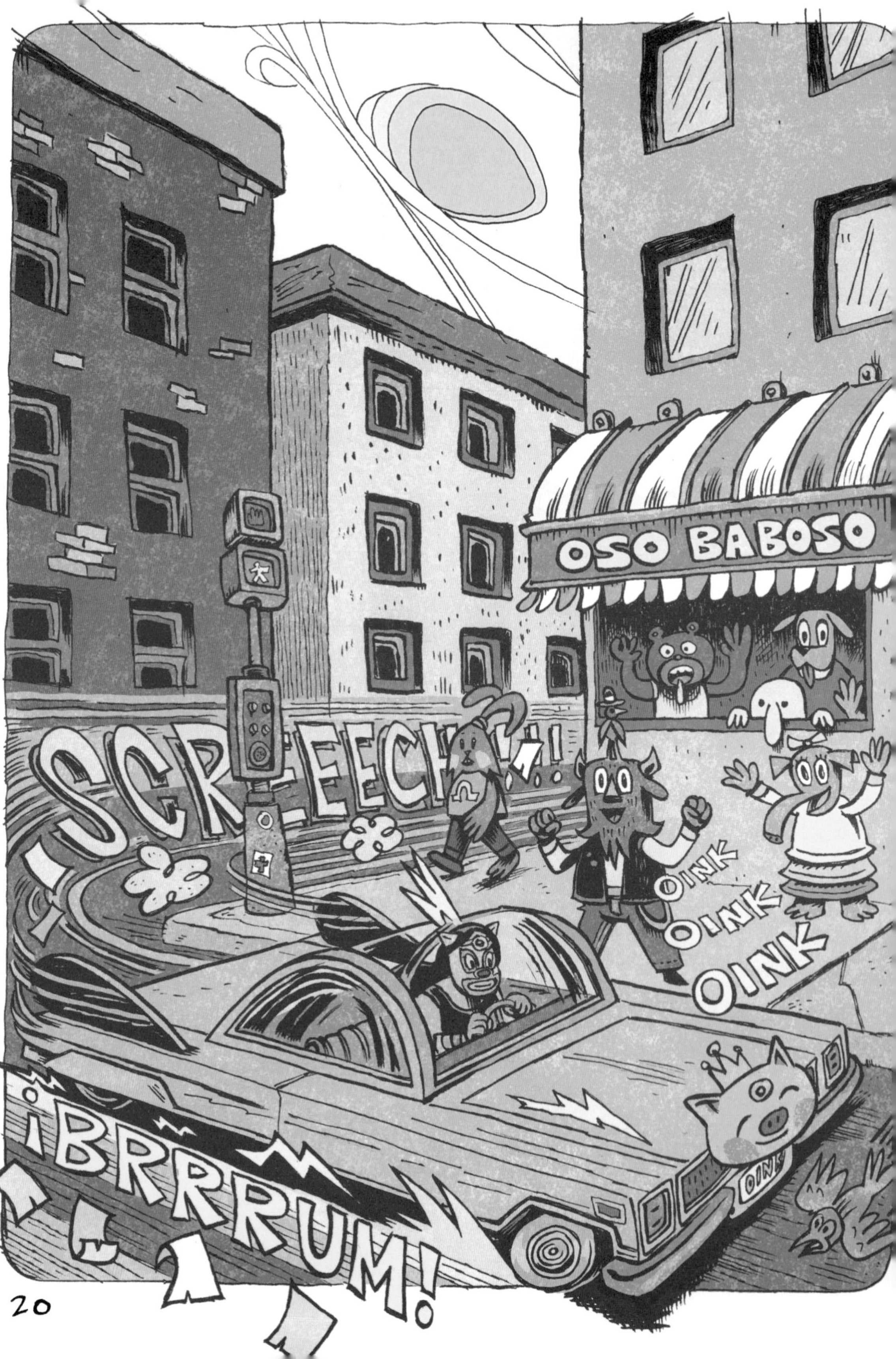
OSO BABOSO
SCREEECH!!!
OINK
OINK
OINK
¡BRRRRUM!
OINK

The sink is full of dirty dishes!

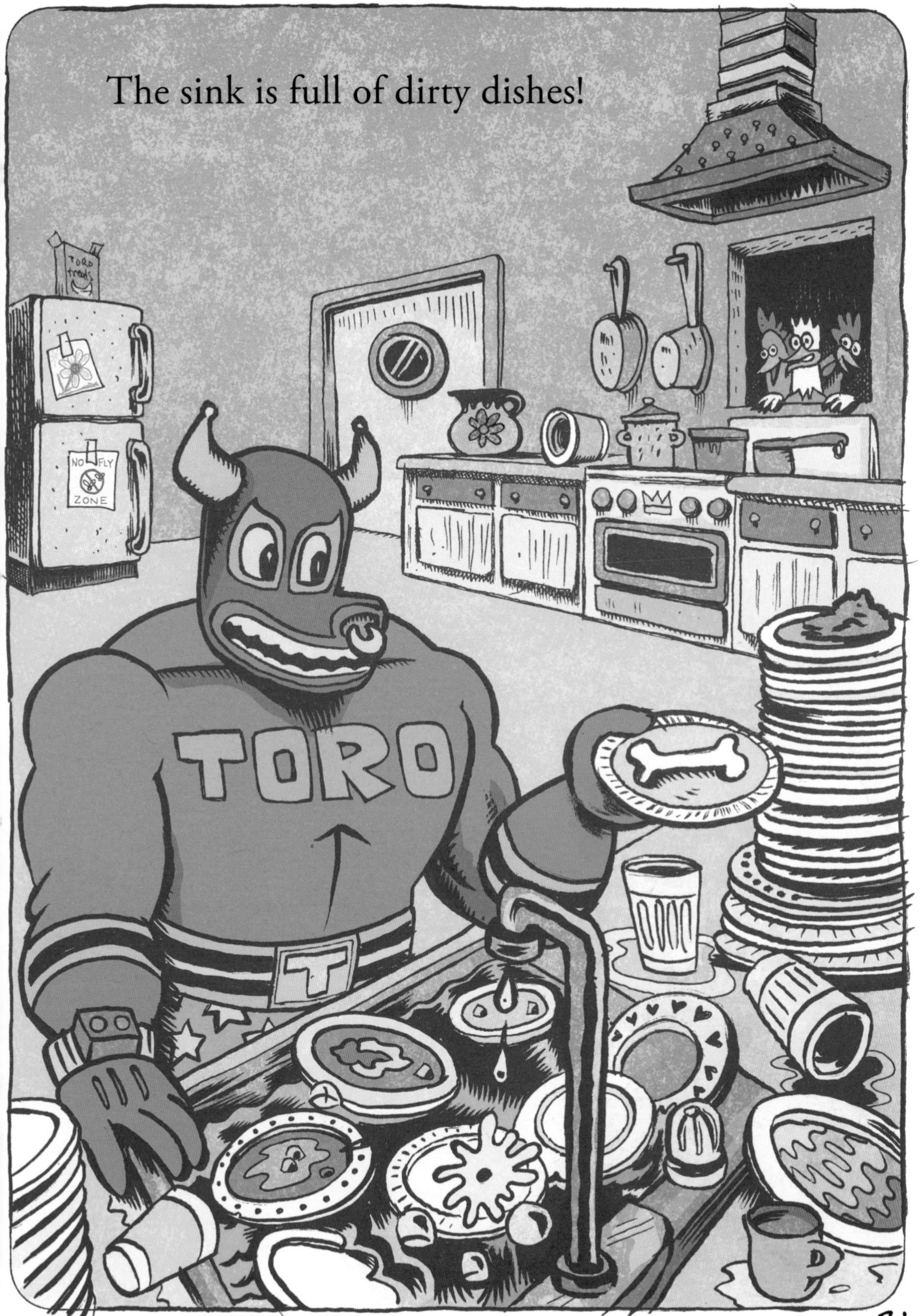
NO FLY ZONE
TORO

And to top it all off, the training chickens got loose.

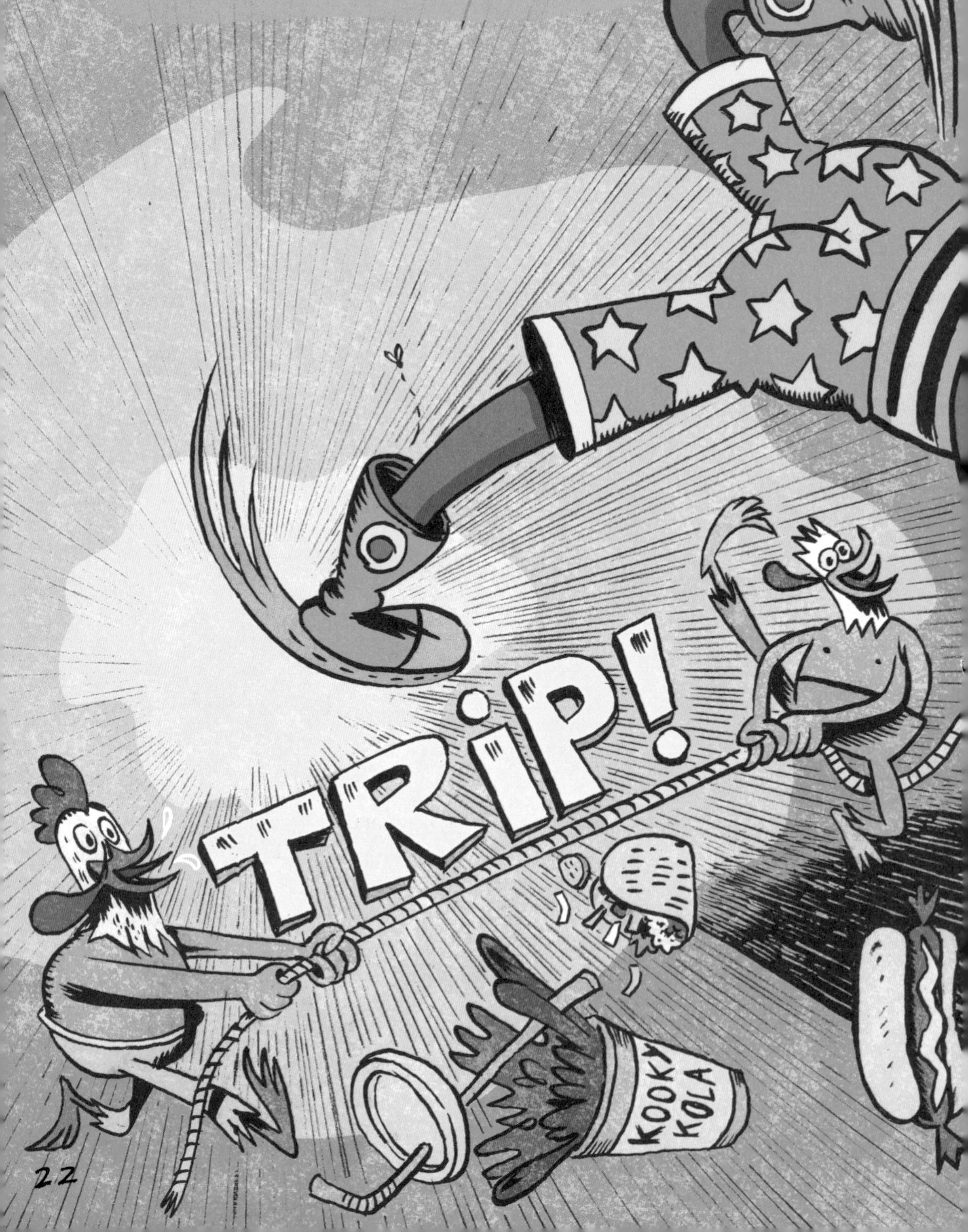
TRIP!
KOOKY KOLA

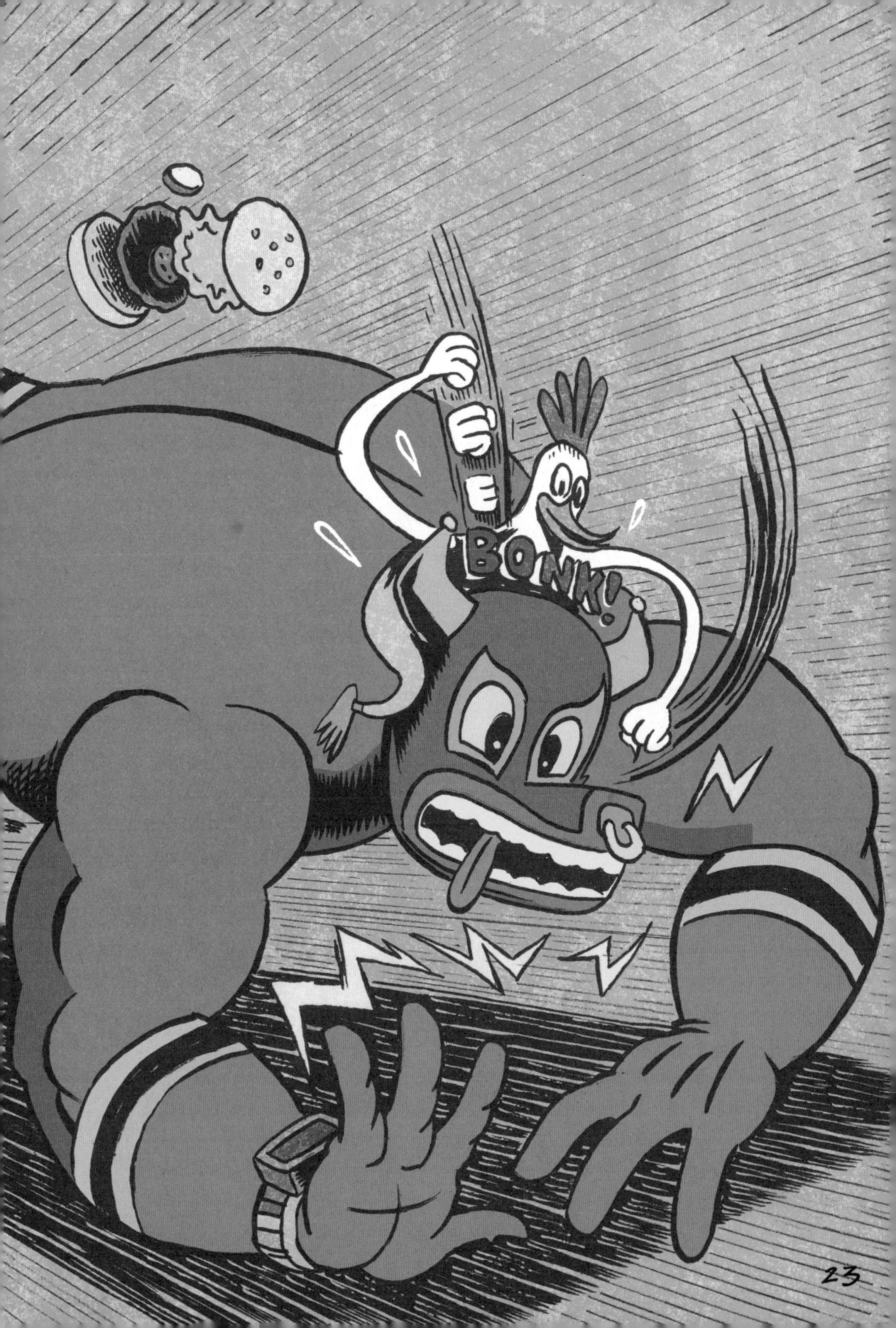
BONK!

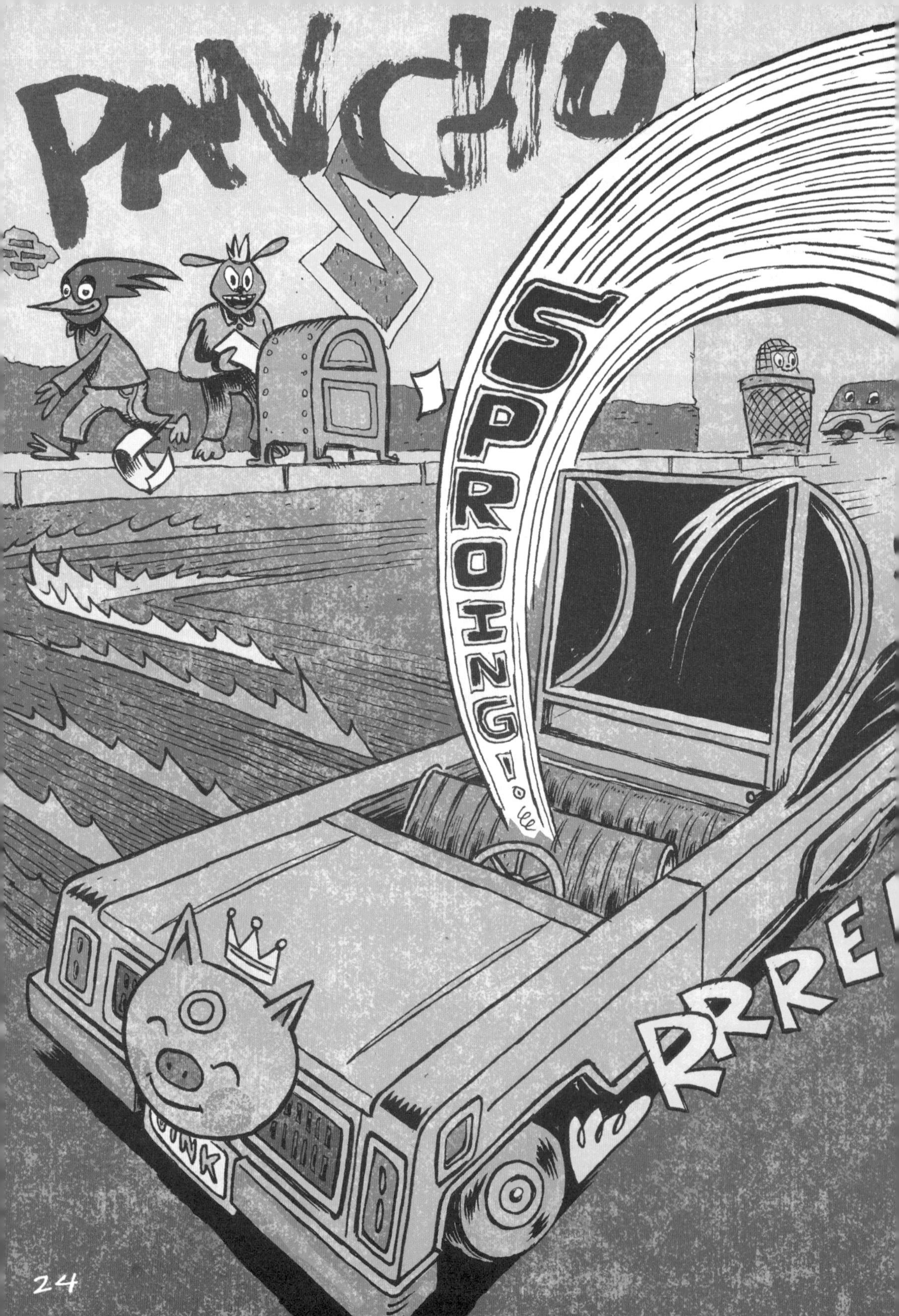
PANCHO
SPROING!
OINK
RRRE

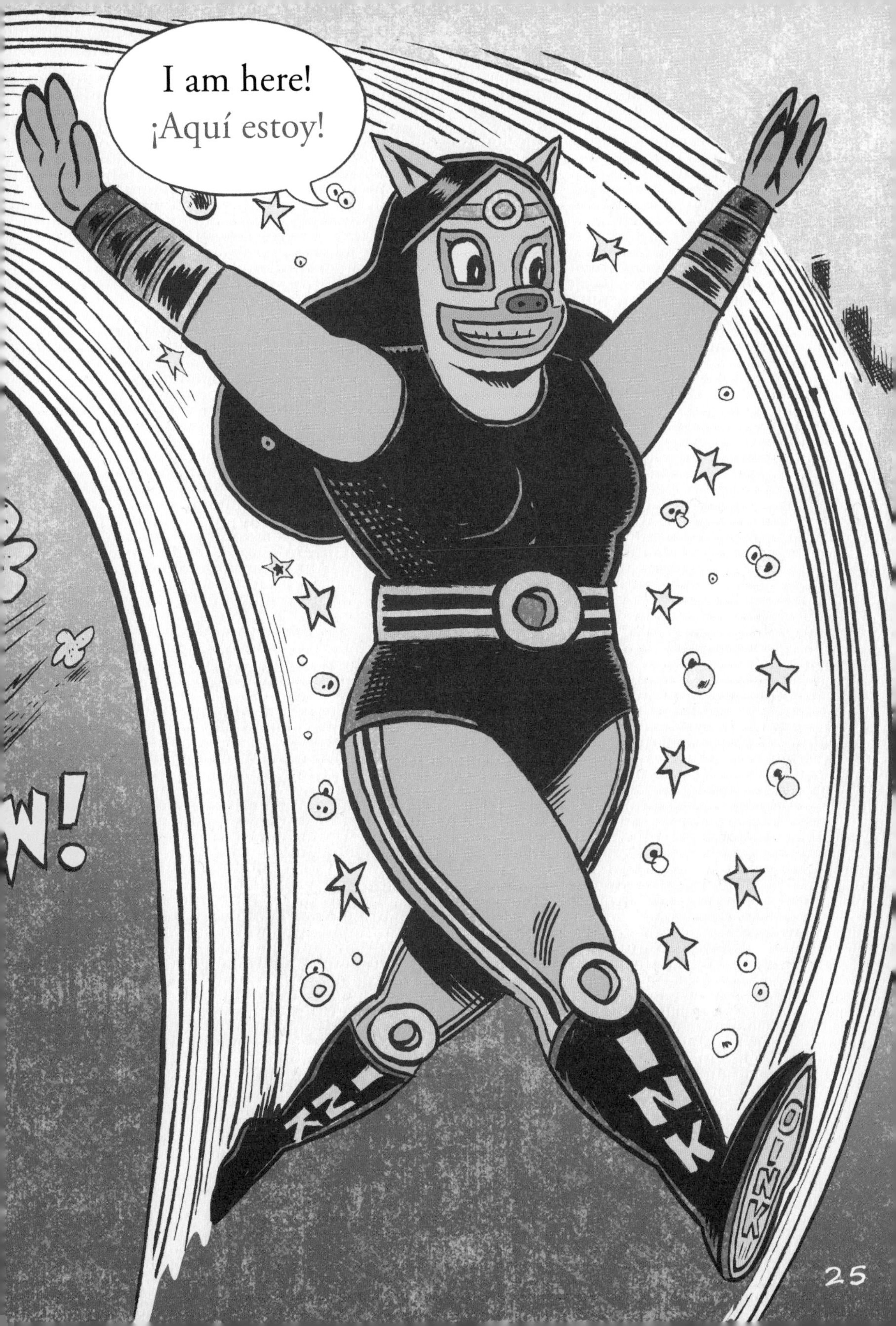
I am here!
¡Aquí estoy!
OINK

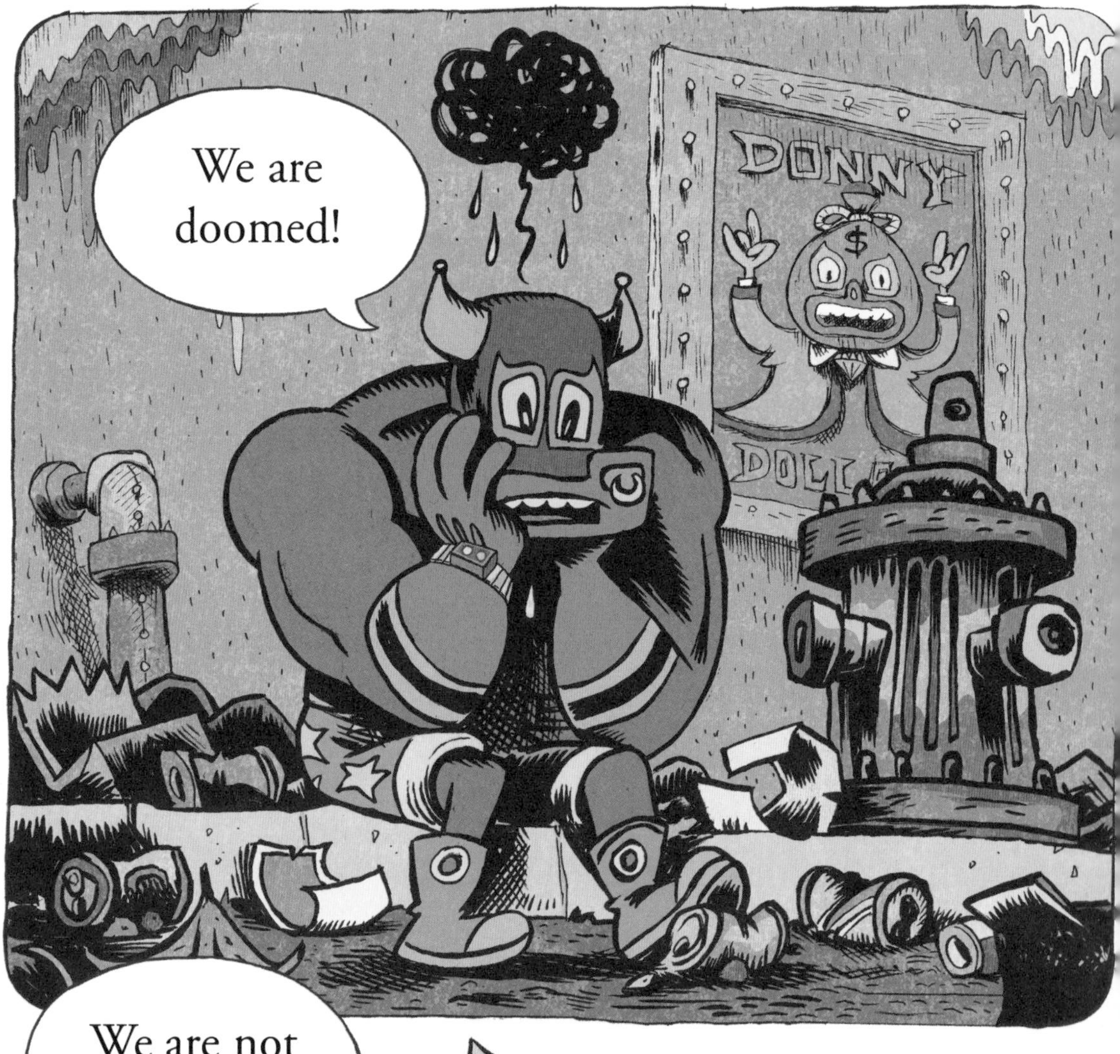
We are doomed!
DONNY

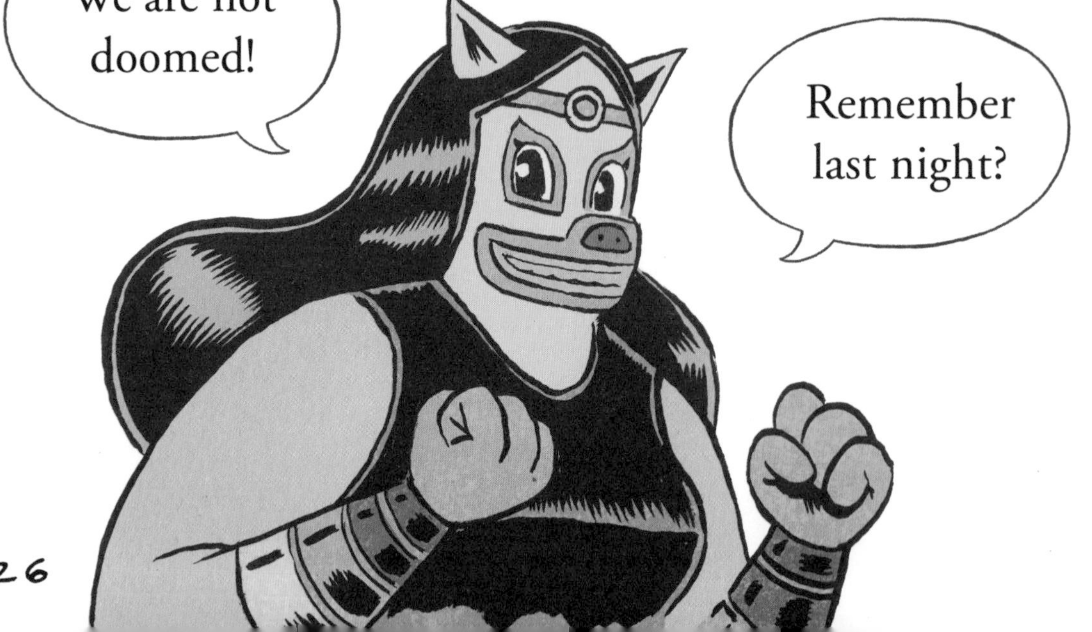
We are not doomed!
Remember last night?

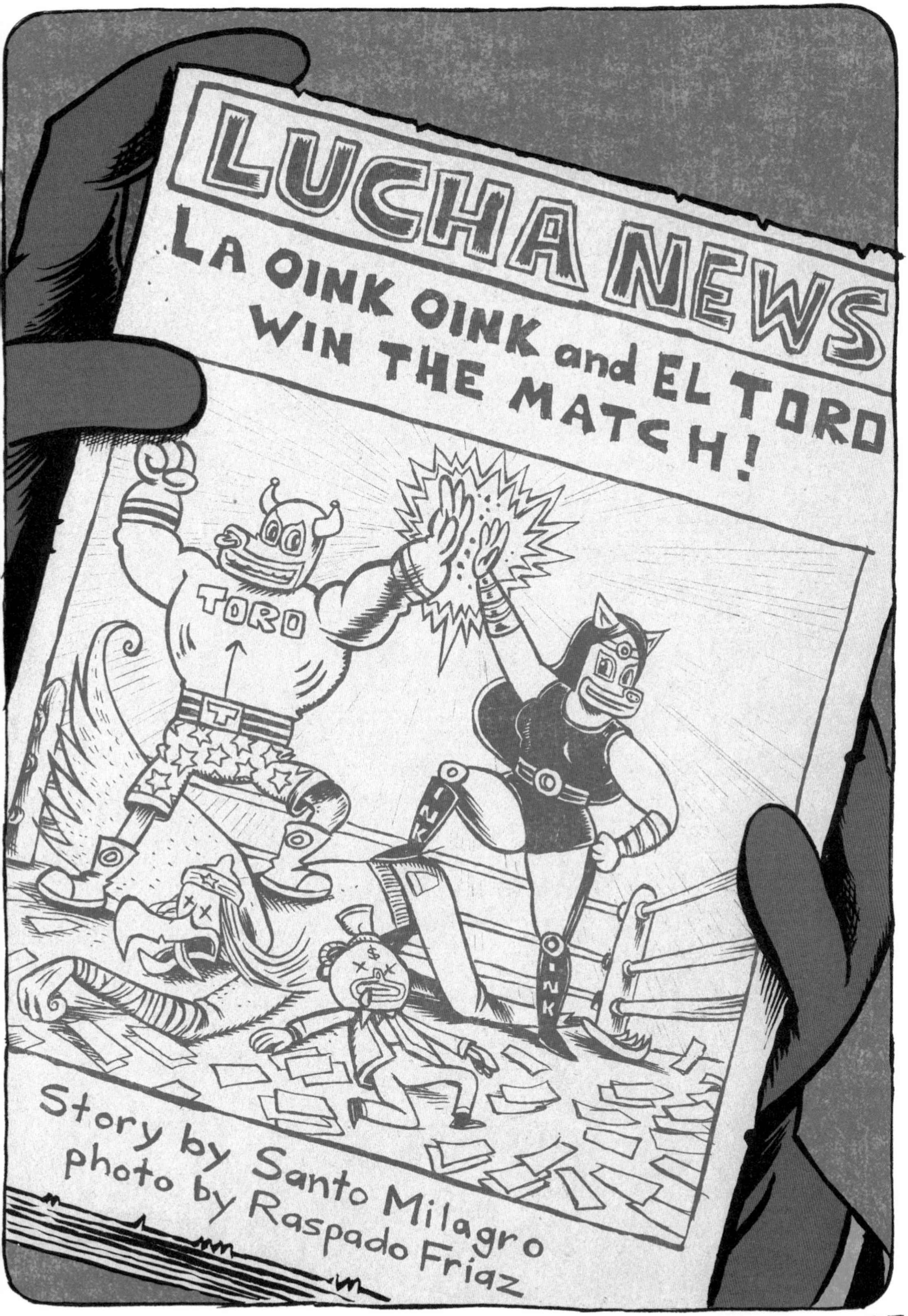
LUCHA NEWS
LA OINK OINK and EL TORO WIN THE MATCH!
TORO
T
OINK
OINK
$
Story by Santo Milagro
photo by Raspado Friaz

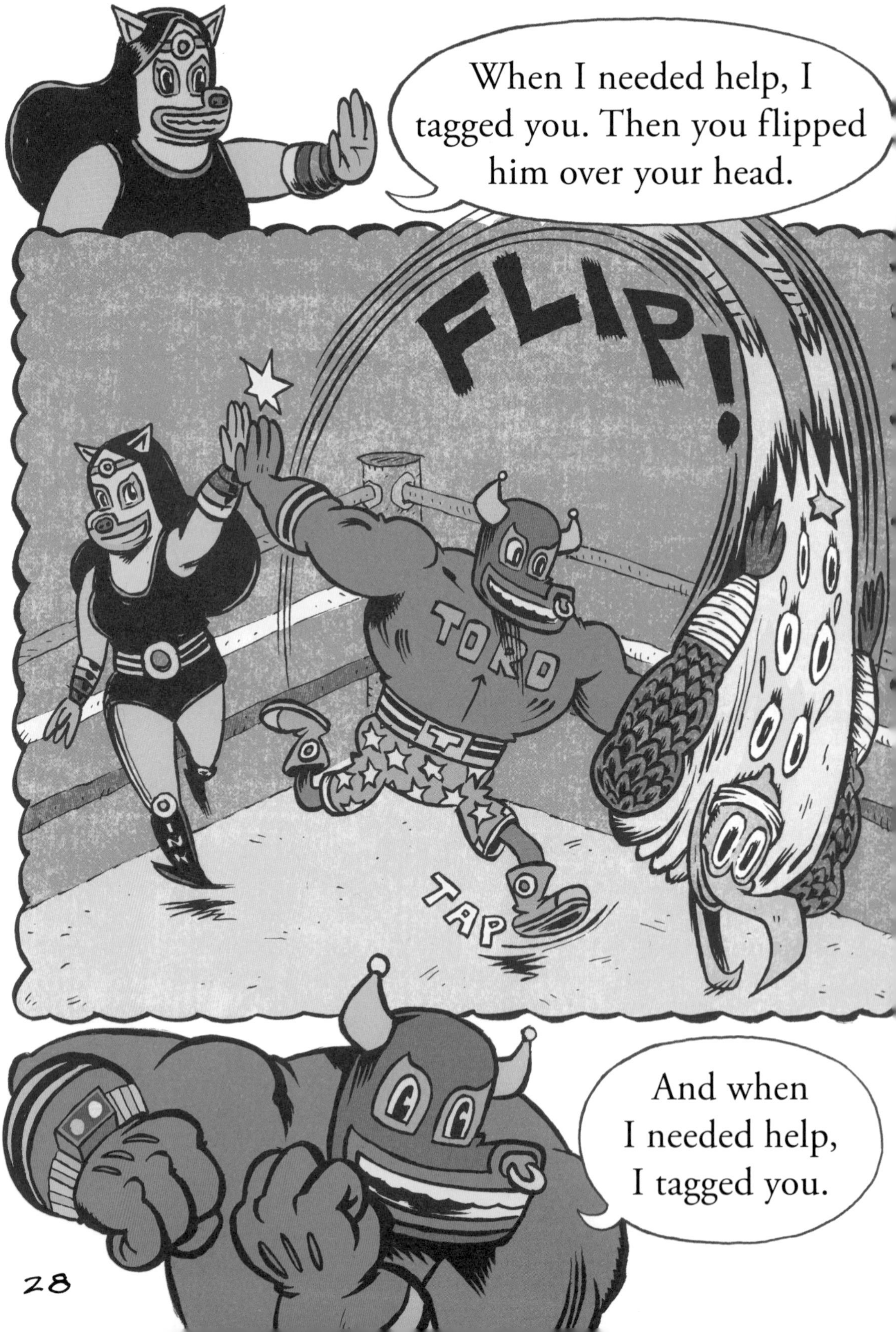
When I needed help, I tagged you. Then you flipped him over your head.
FLIP!
TORO
TAP
And when I needed help, I tagged you.

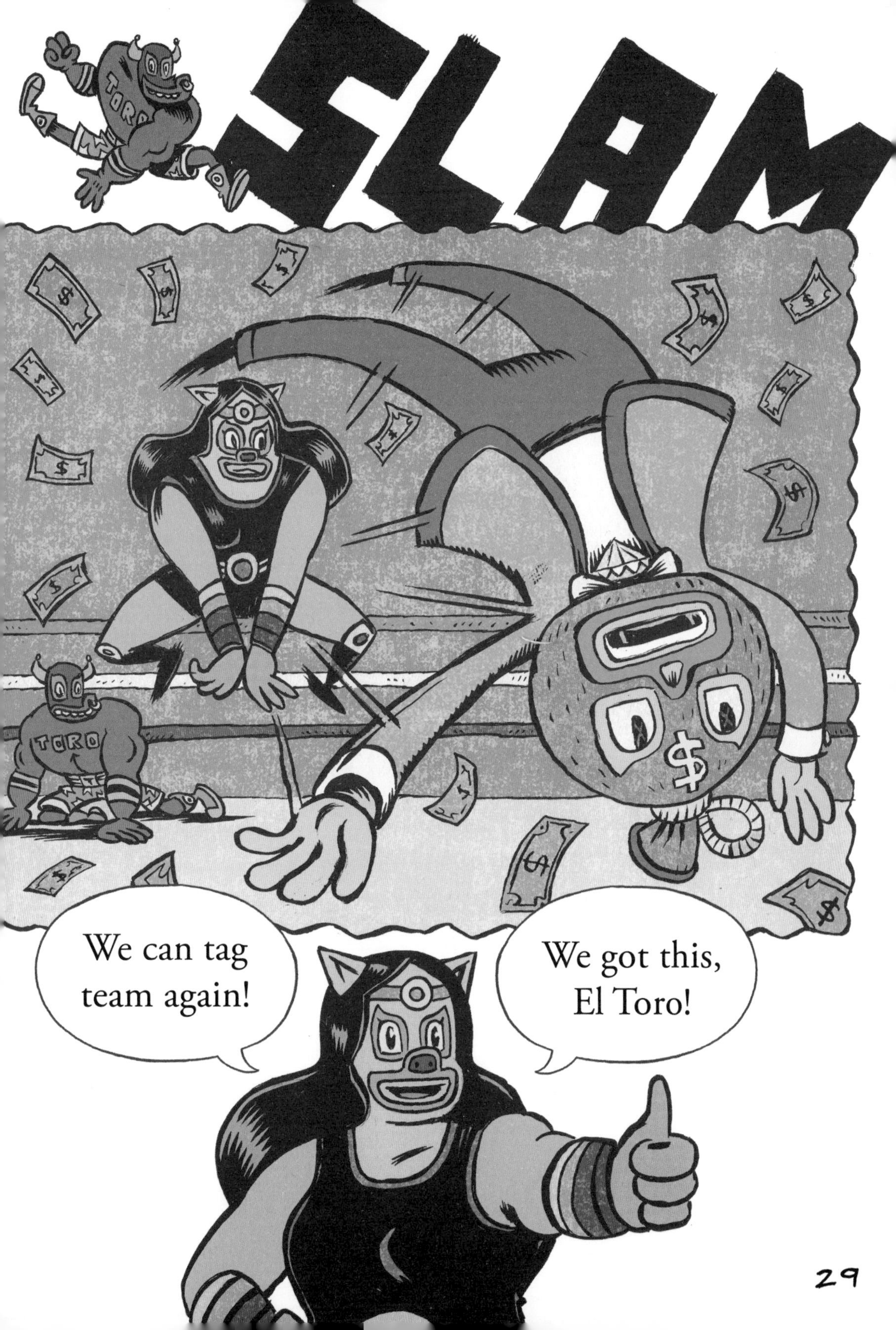
SLAM
TORO
TORO
We can tag team again!
We got this, El Toro!

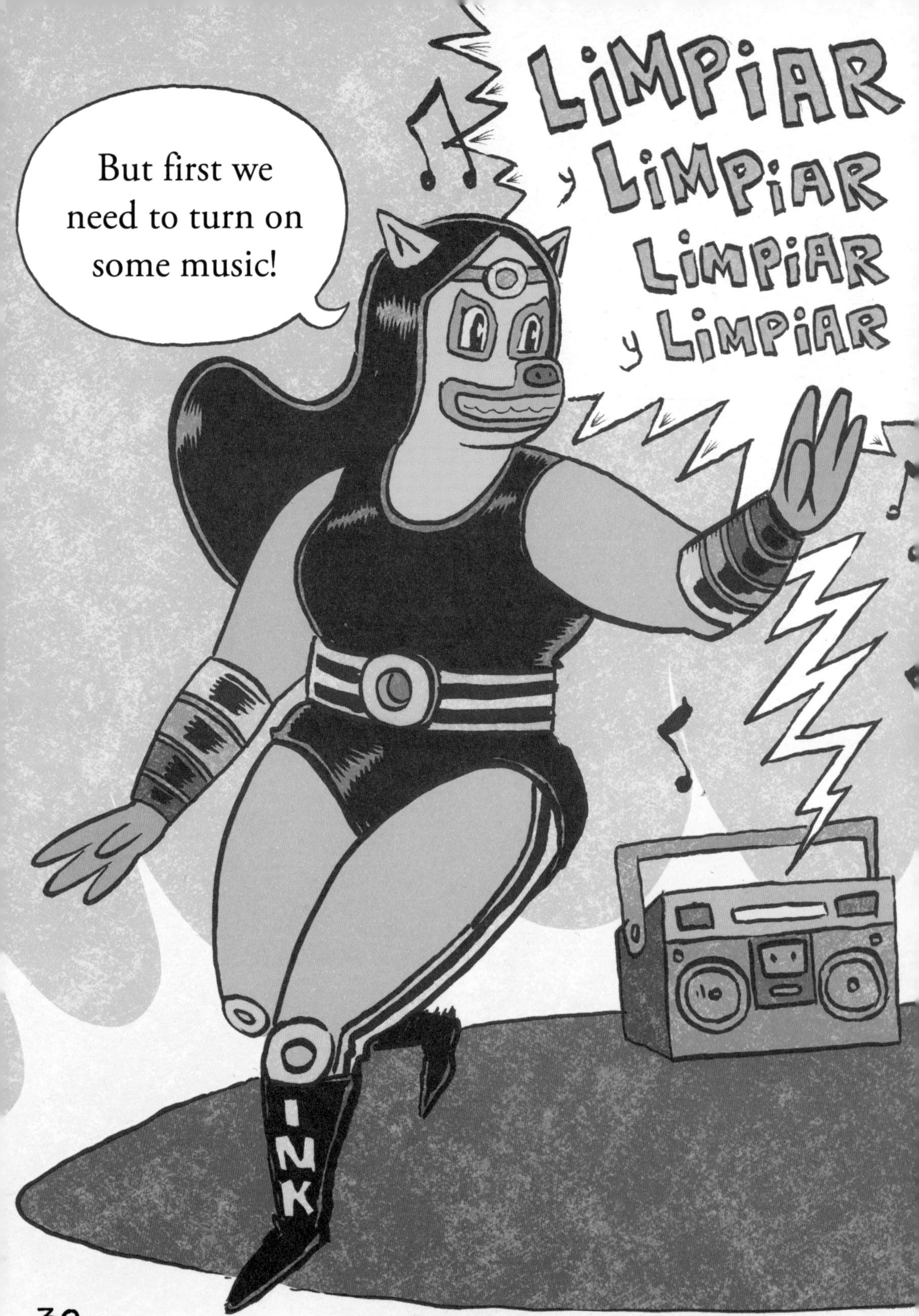
But first we need to turn on some music!
LIMPIAR y LIMPIAR LIMPIAR y LIMPIAR
INK

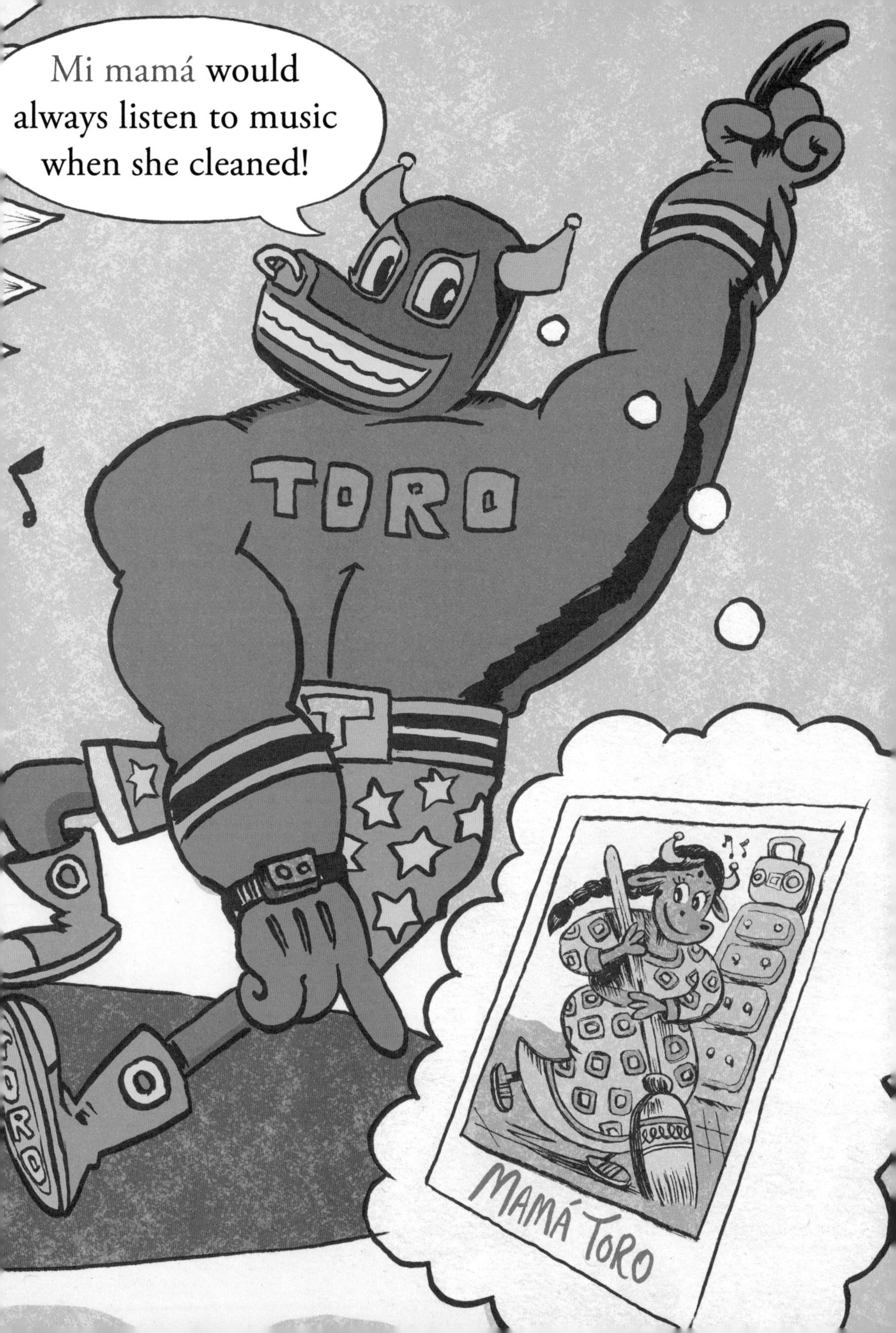
Mi mamá would always listen to music when she cleaned!
TORO
TORO
MAMÁ TORO

La Oink Oink grabs la escoba and dances around the room.

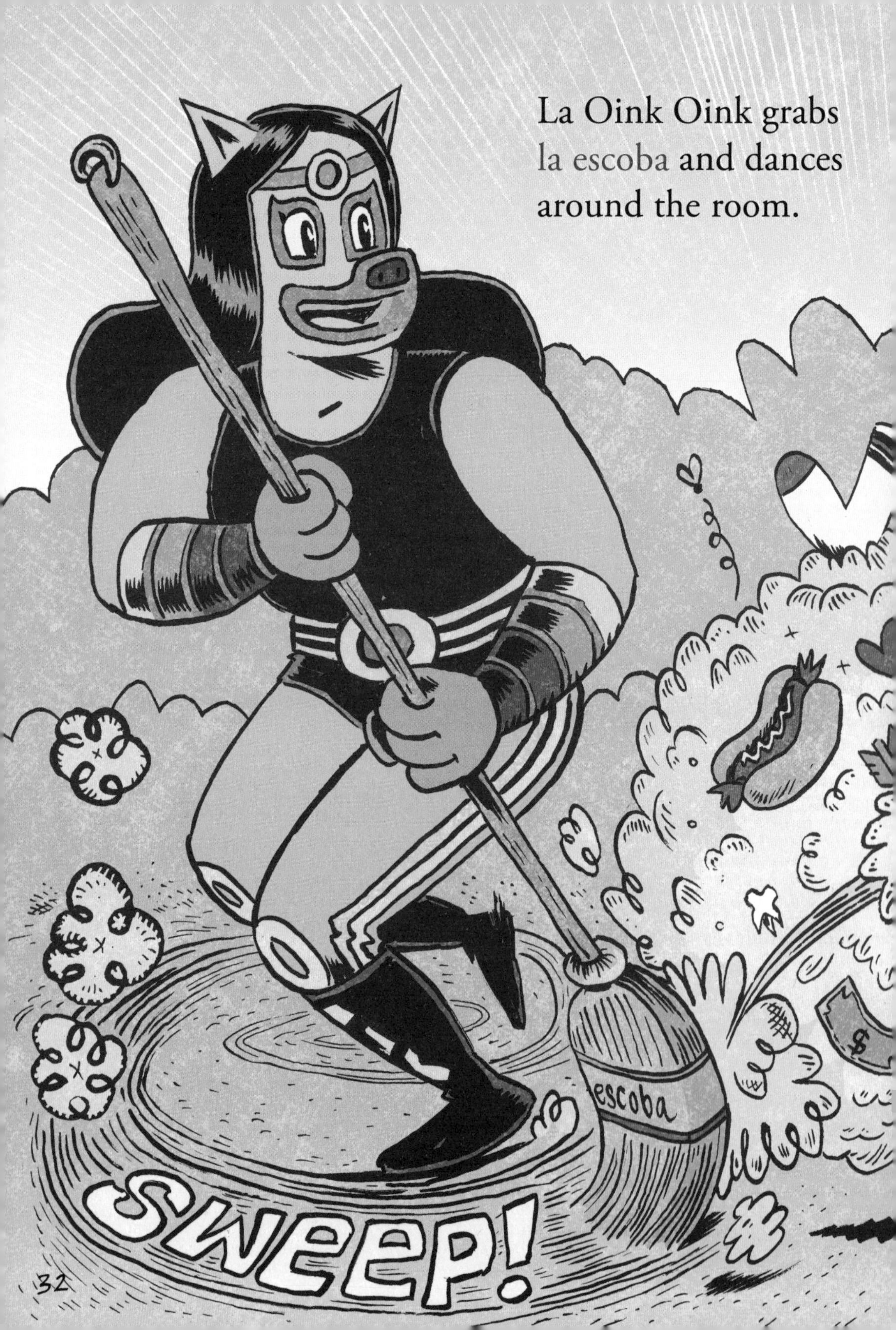
escoba
SWEEP!

El Toro uses the dustpan
to gather up the trash.

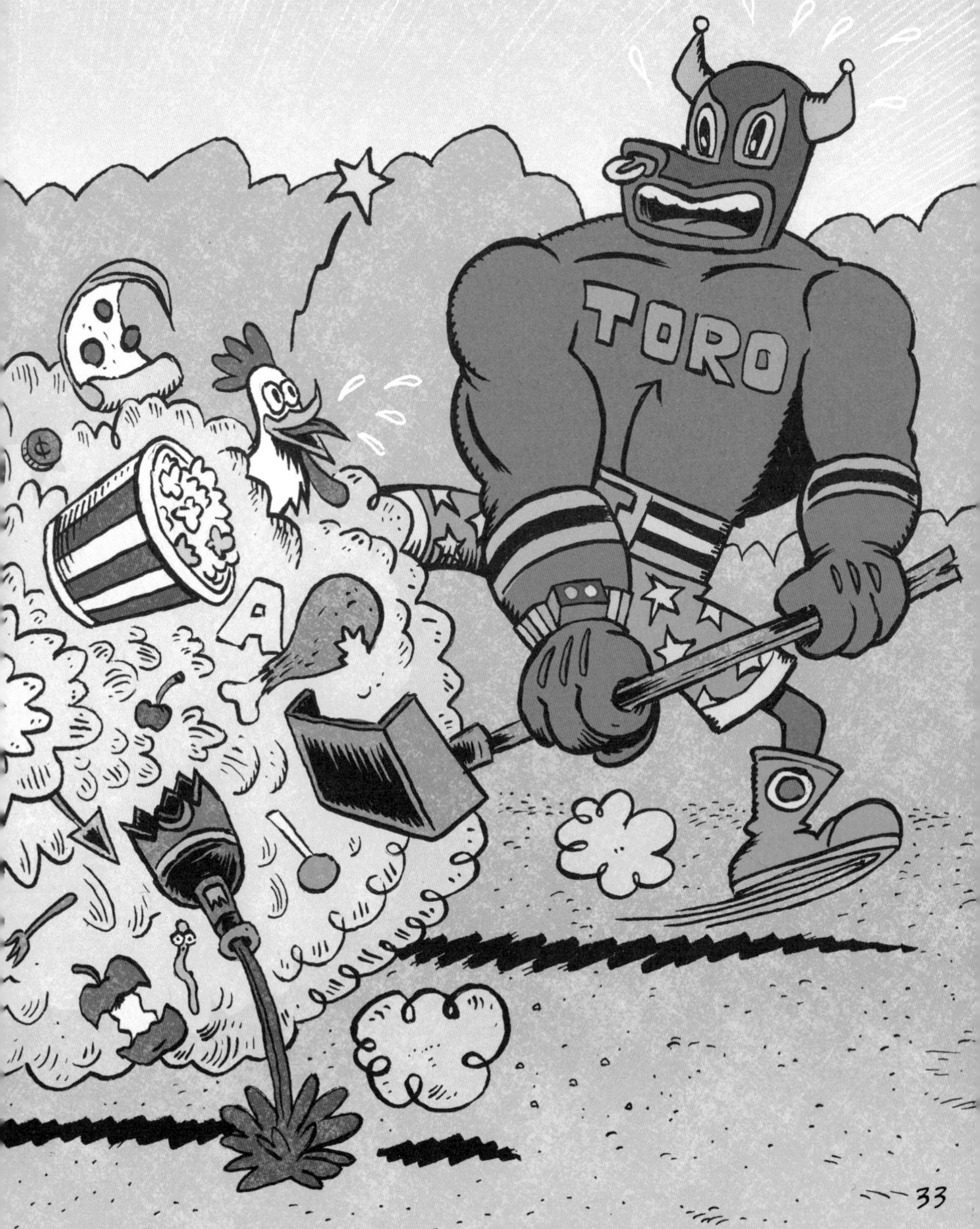

TORO
A

El Toro mops

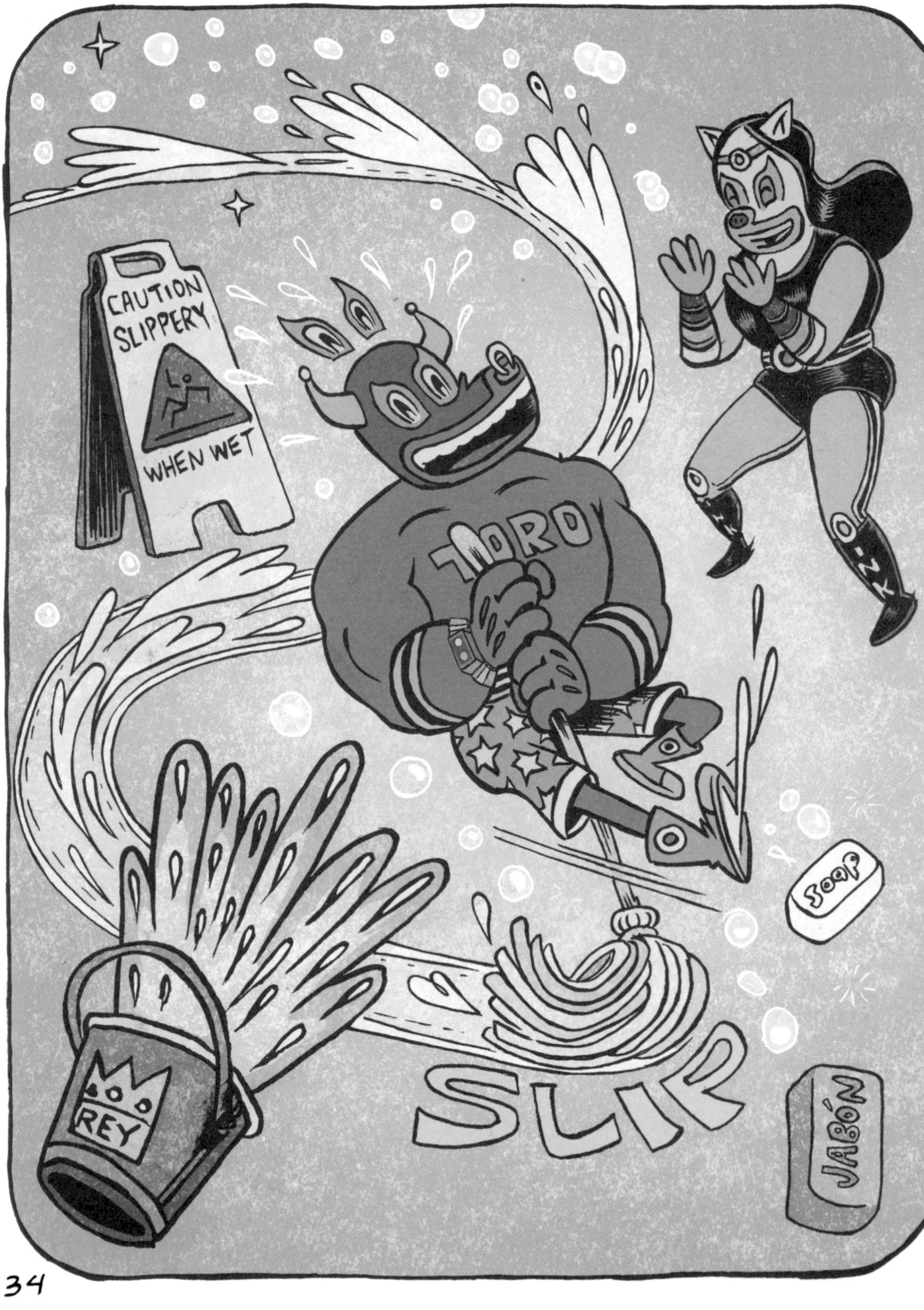

CAUTION
SLIPPERY
WHEN WET
TORO
SOAP
SLIP
REY
JABÓN

and La Oink Oink blows the floor dry.

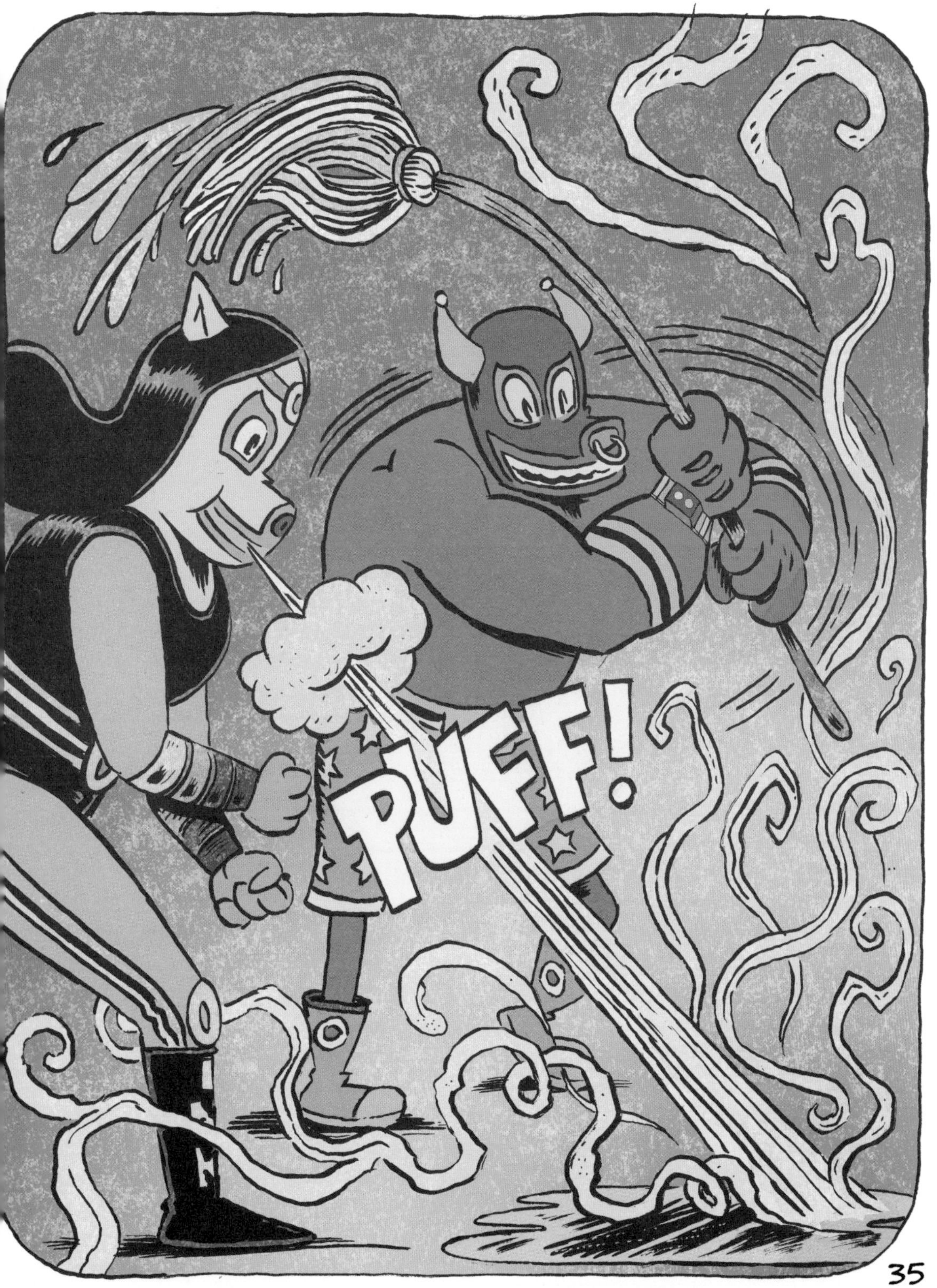
PUFF!

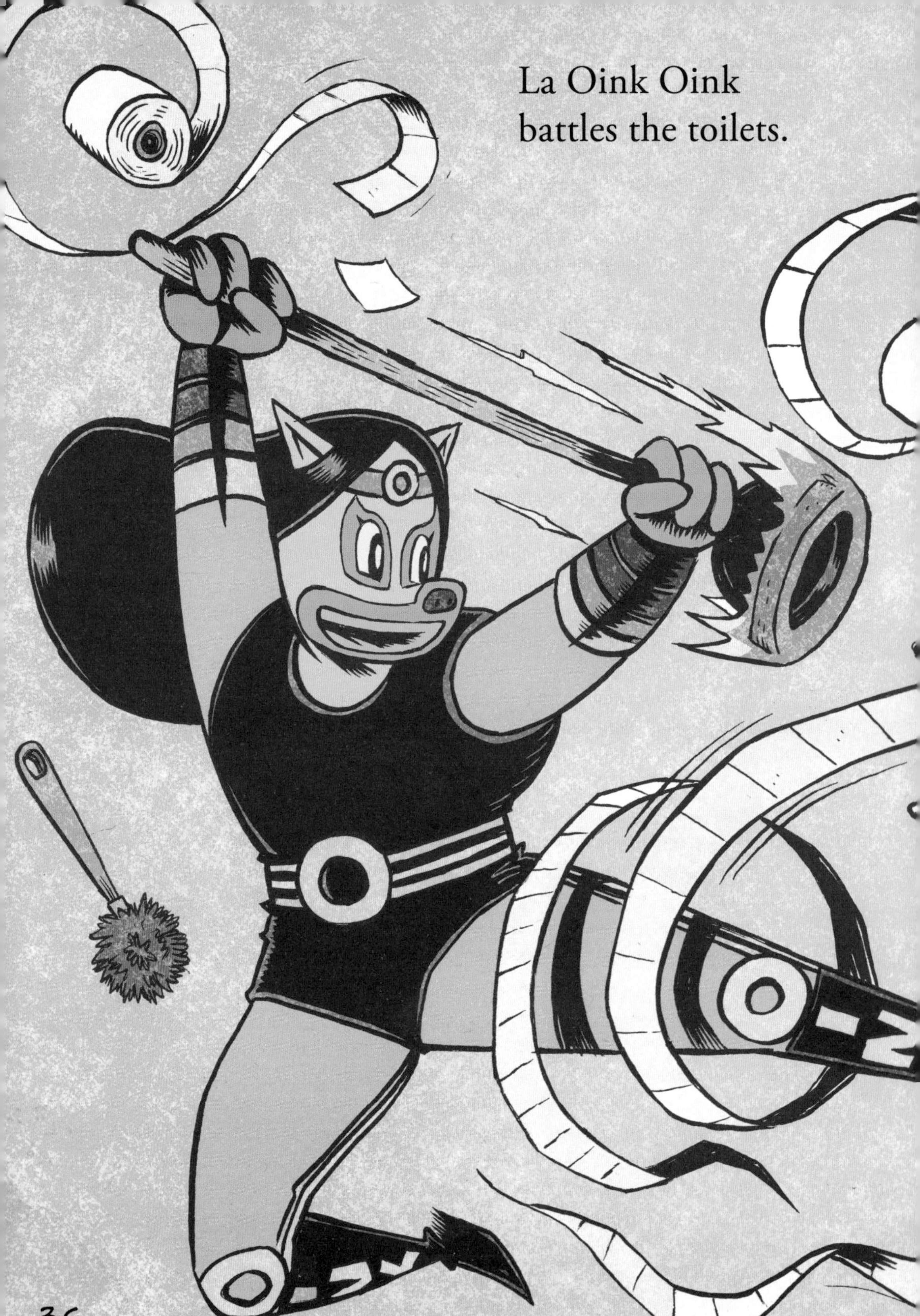
La Oink Oink battles the toilets.

El Toro holds
his nose and jiggles
the handle.

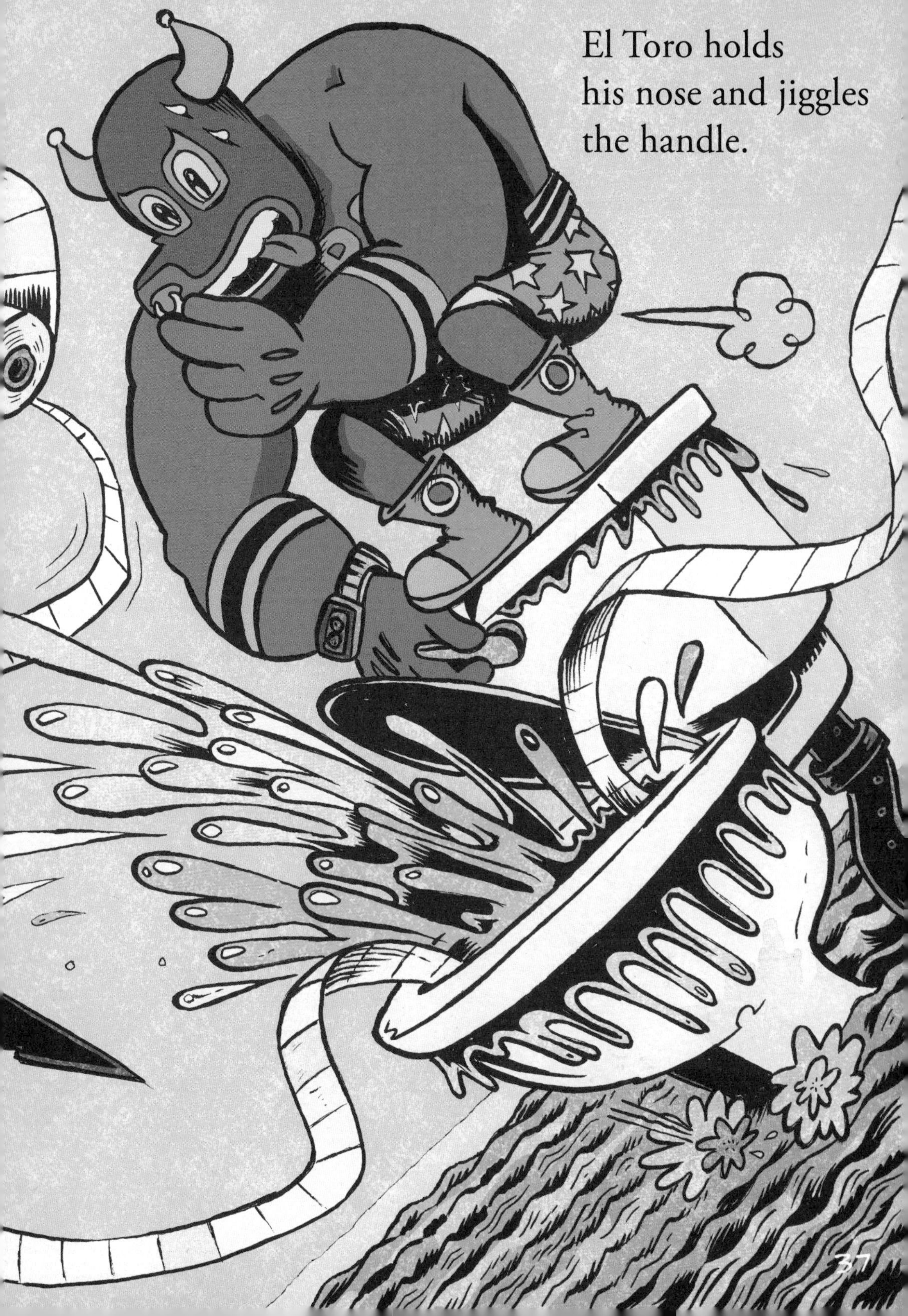

El Toro stretches the canvas and
La Oink Oink tightens the ropes!

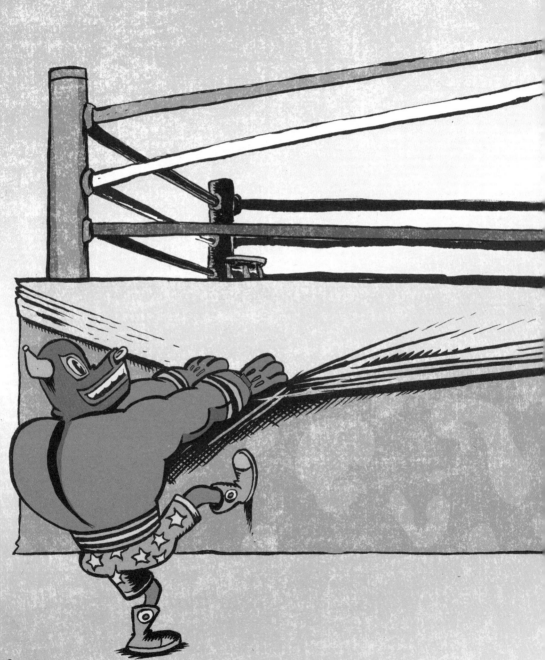

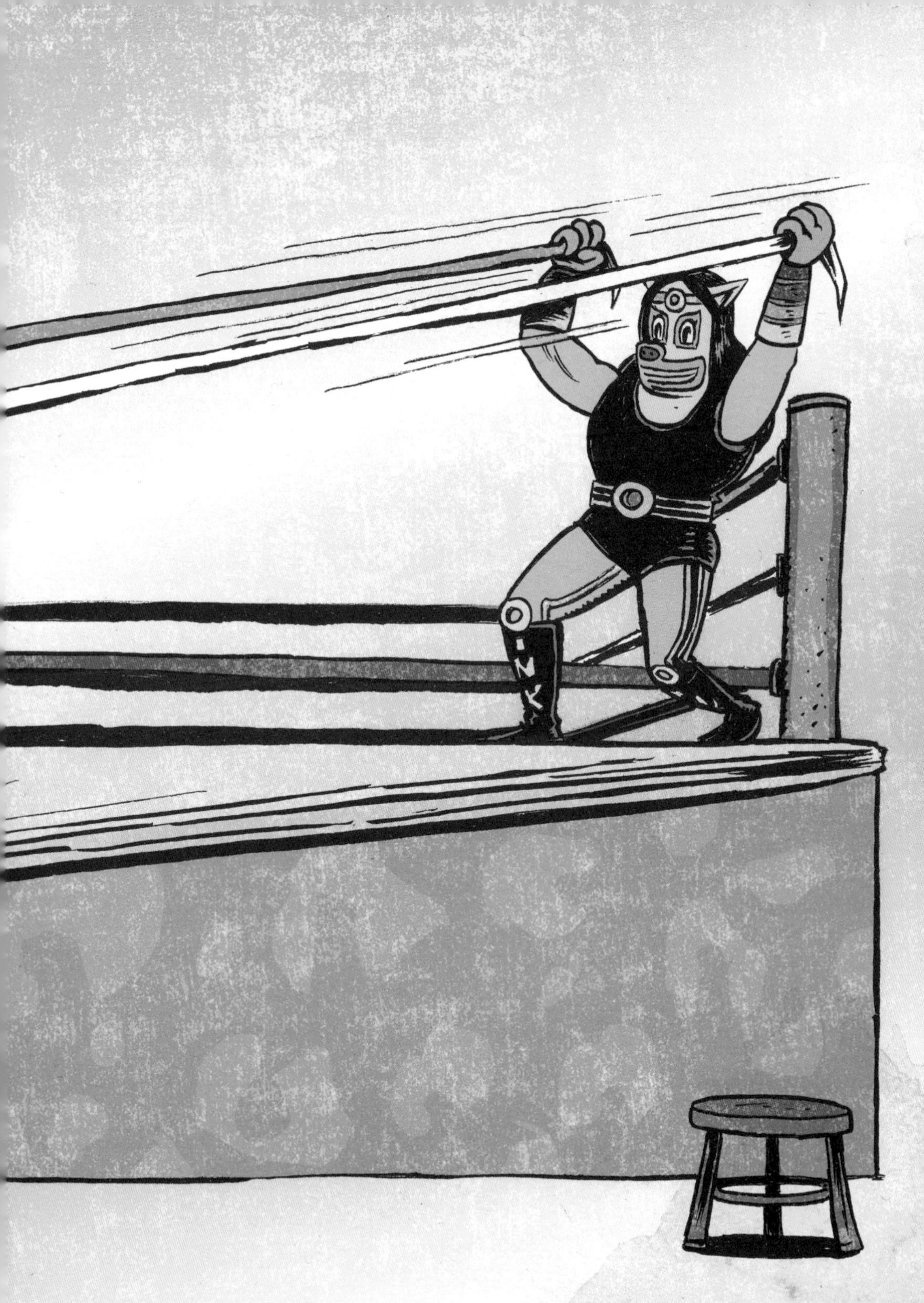
INK

El Toro washes
the dishes.

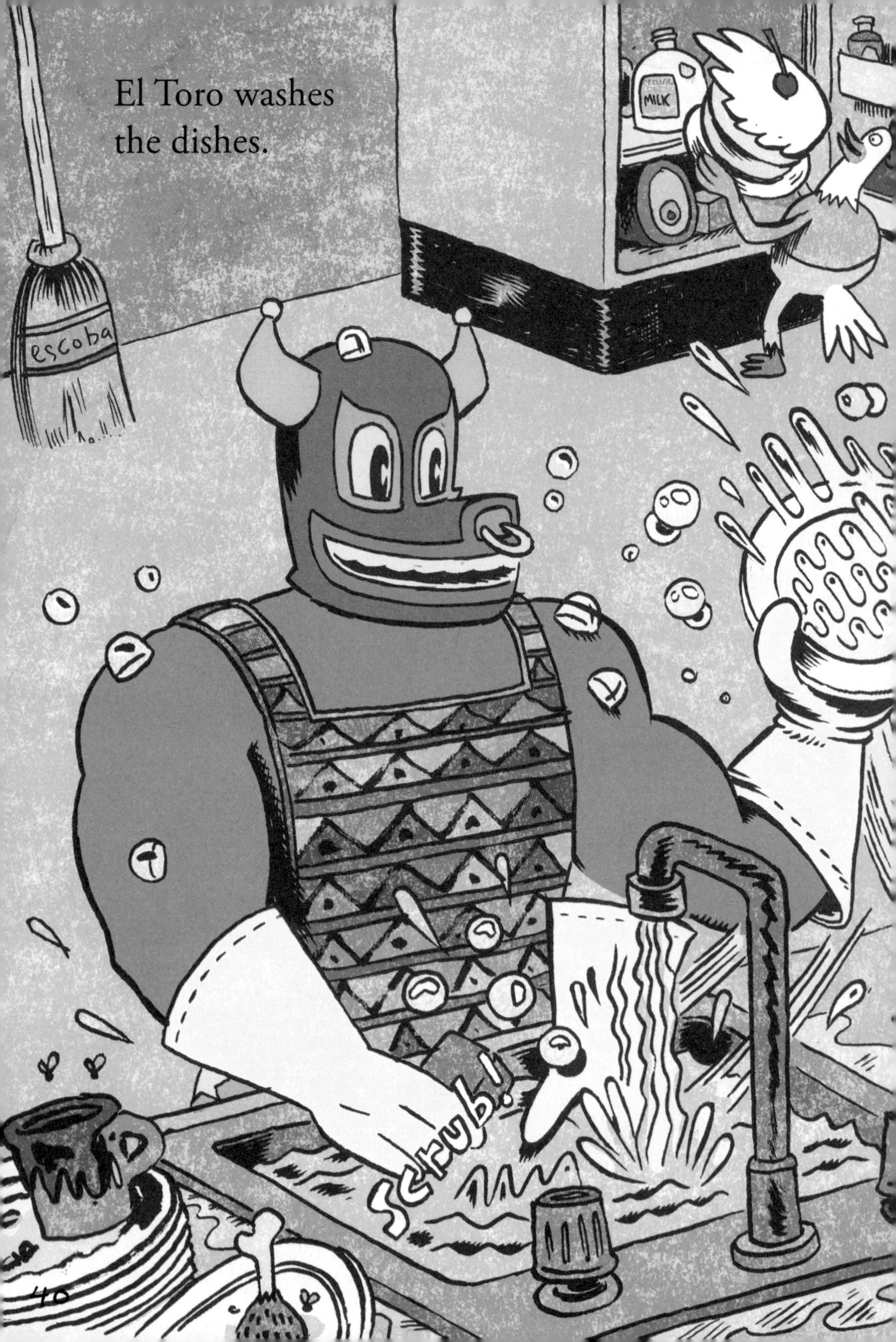
escoba
MILK
scrub!

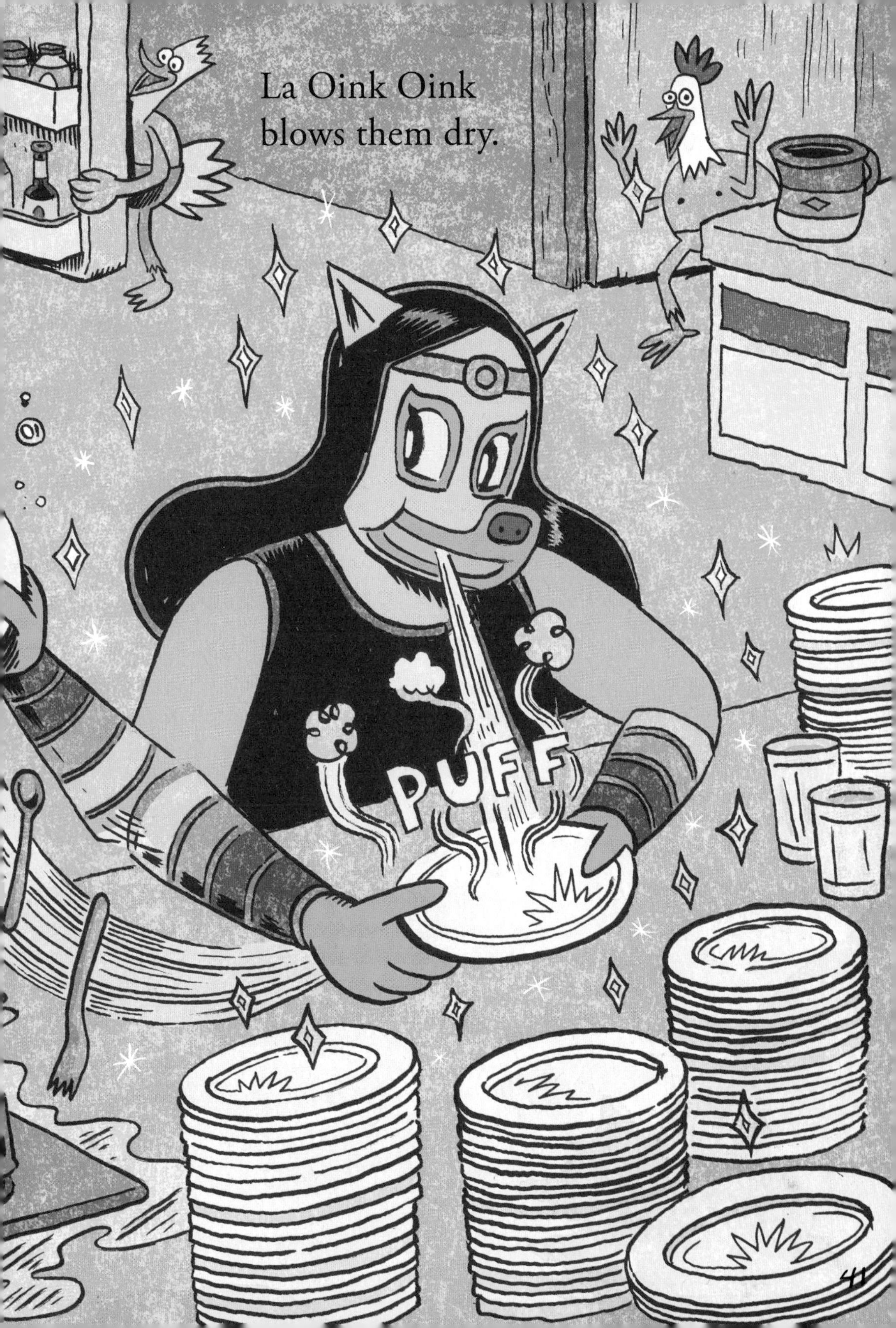
La Oink Oink
blows them dry.
PUFF

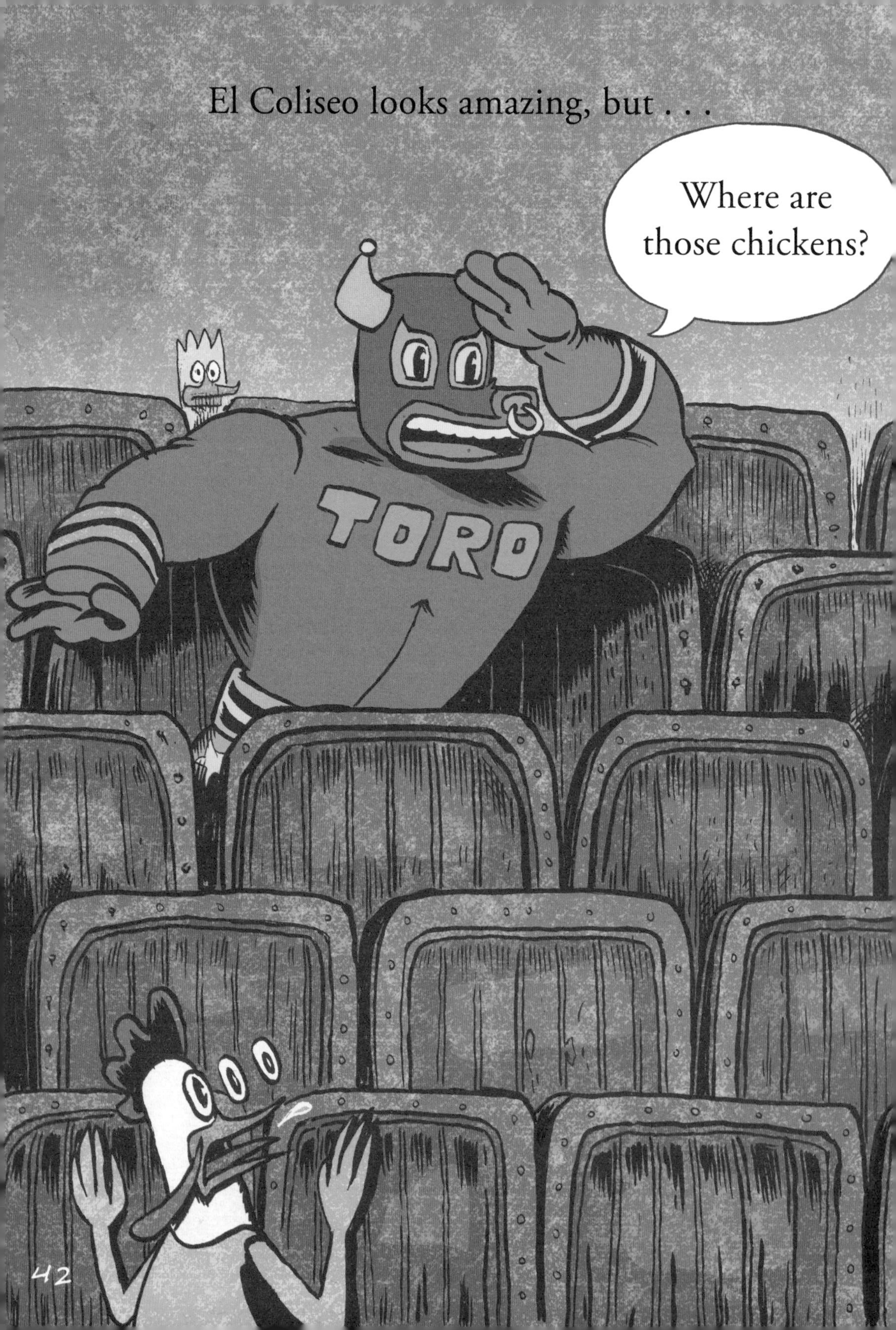
El Coliseo looks amazing, but . . .
Where are those chickens?
TORO

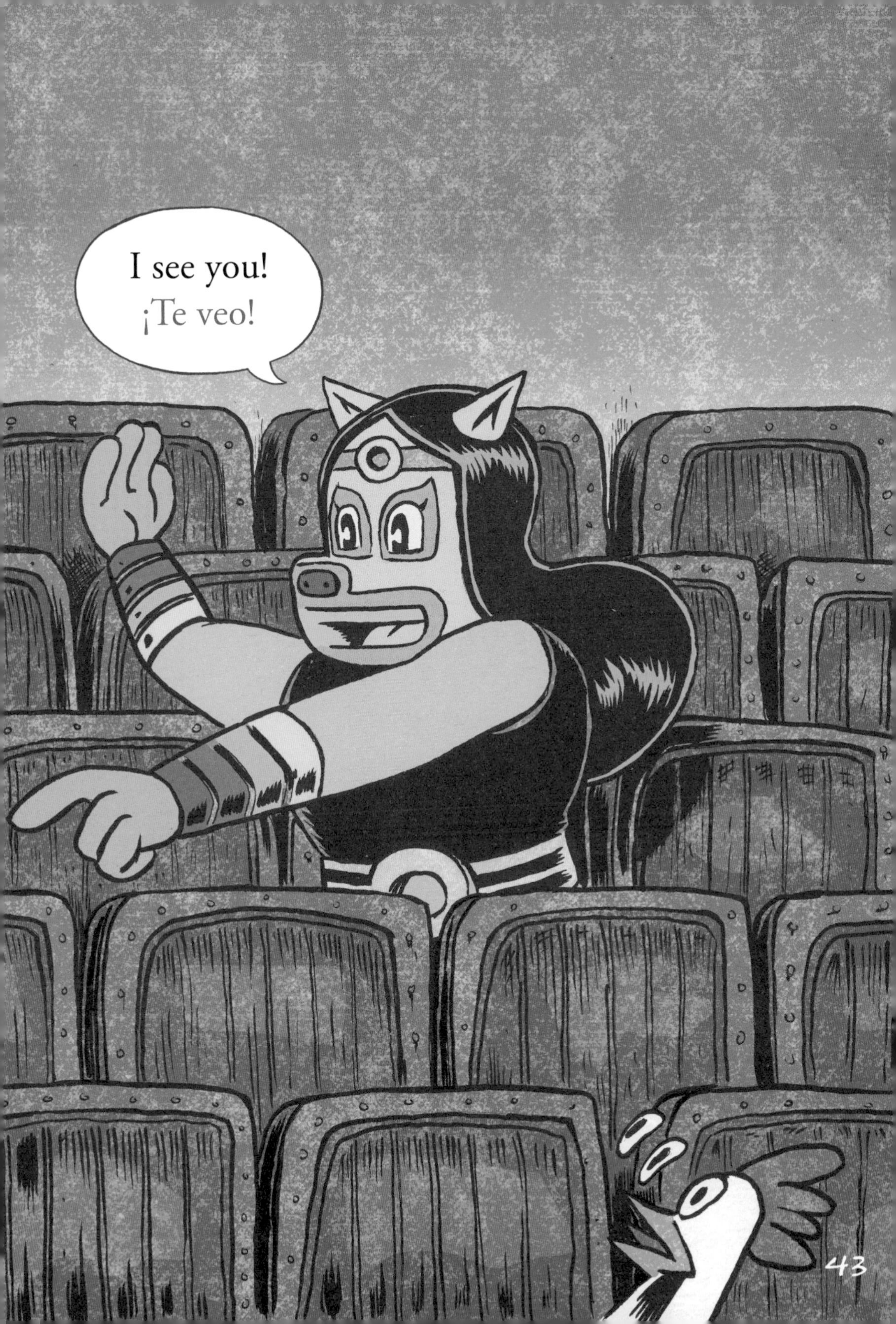
I see you!
¡Te veo!

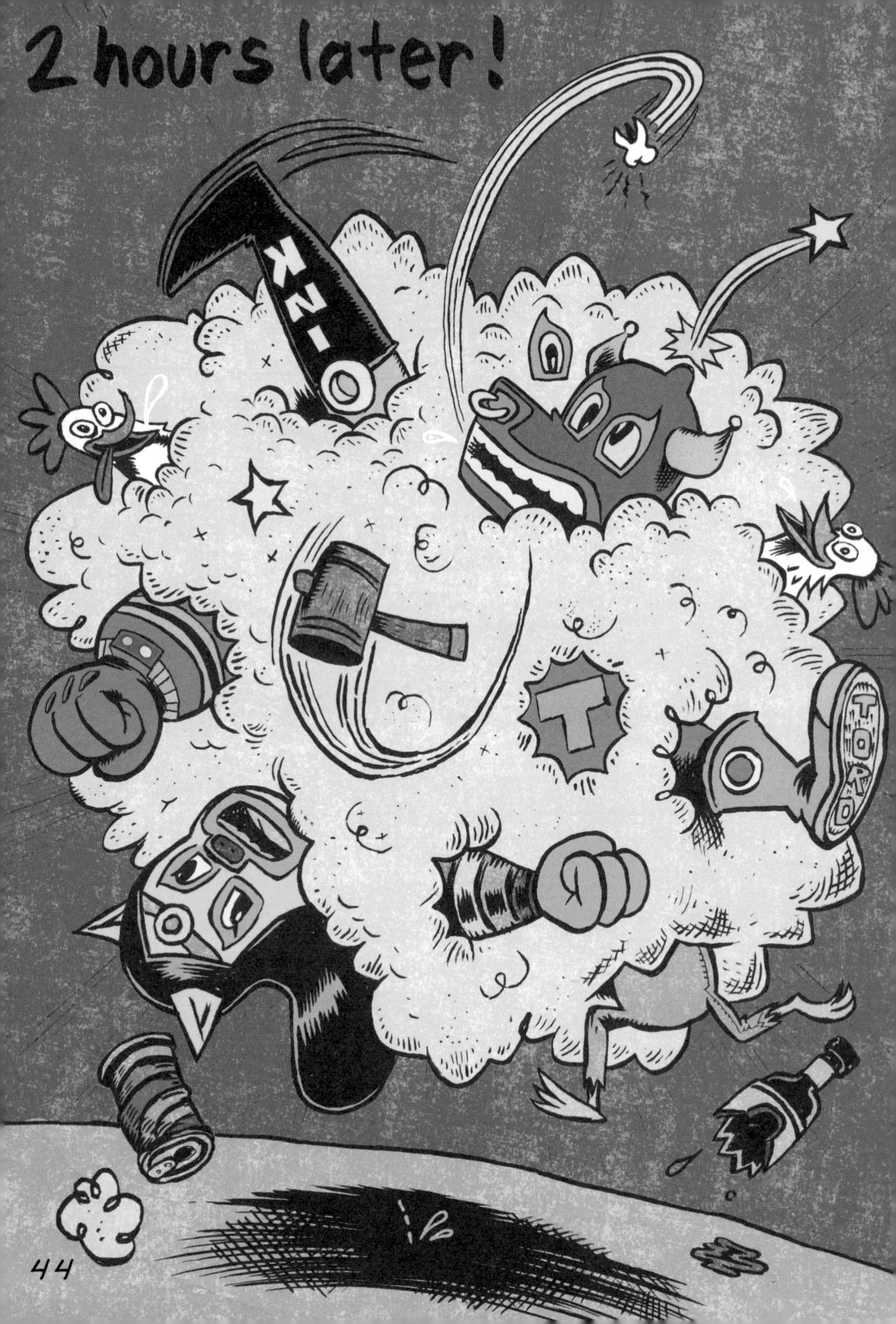
2 hours later!
INK
T
TORO

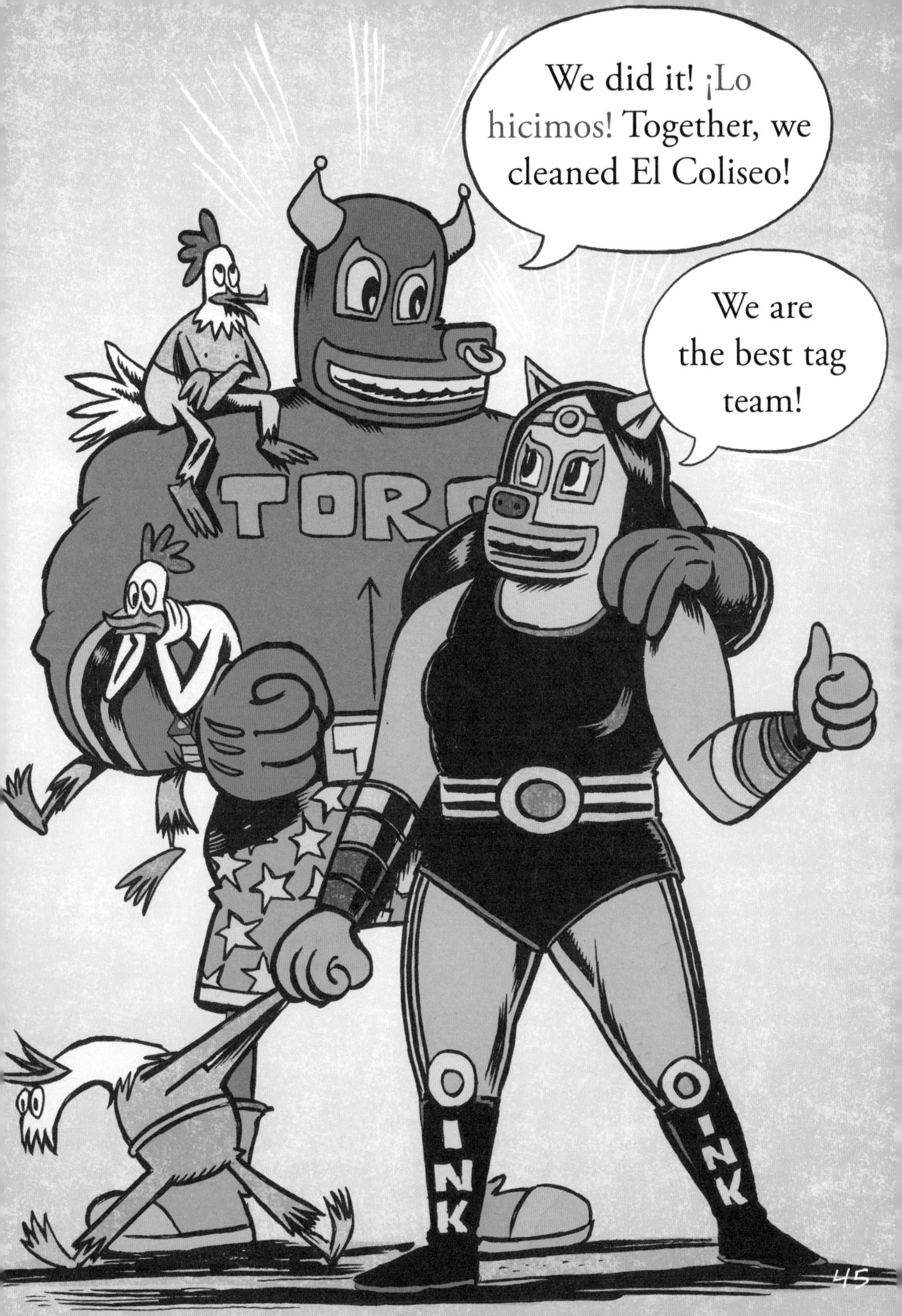
We did it! ¡Lo hicimos! Together, we cleaned El Coliseo!
We are the best tag team!
TORO
INK
INK

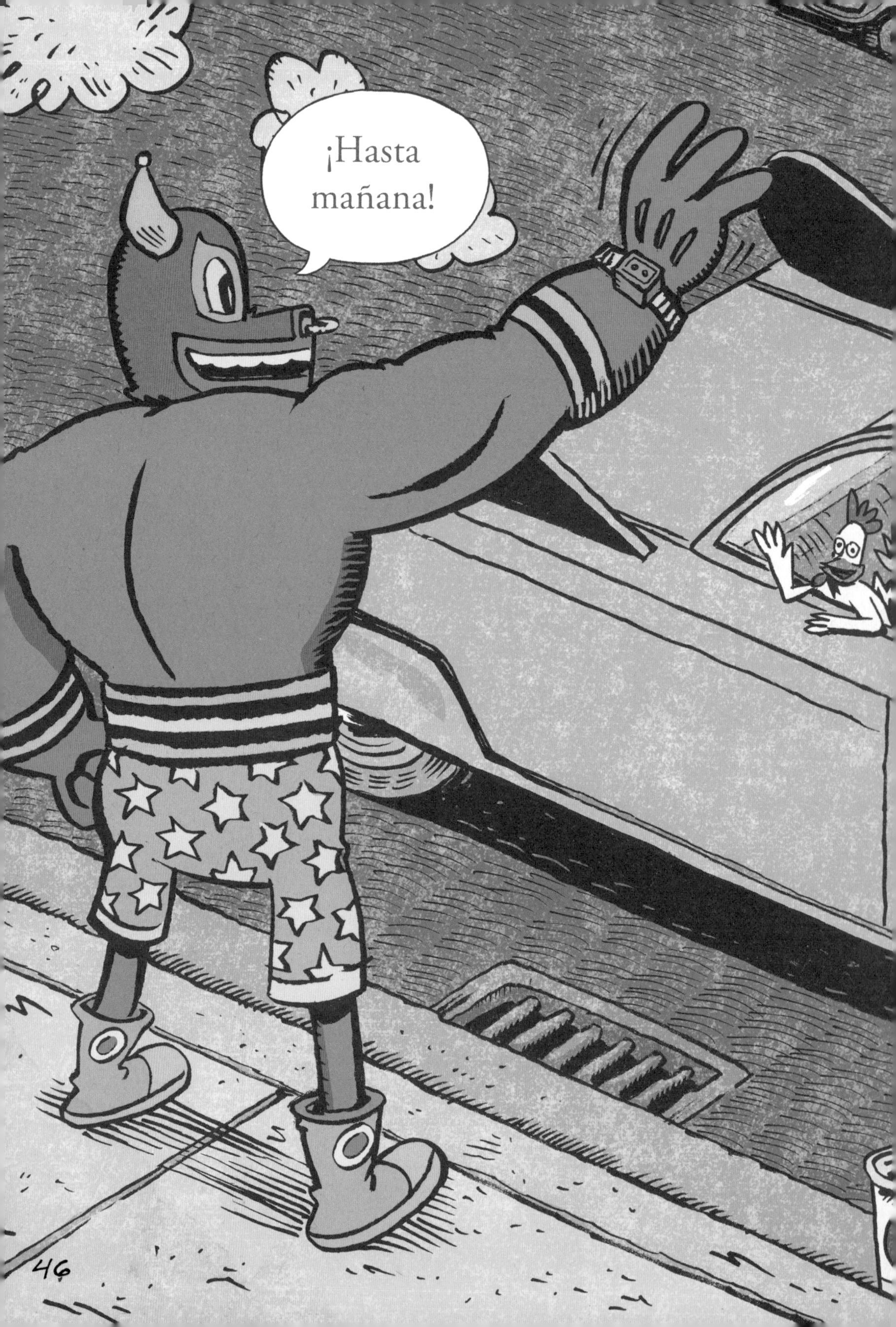
¡Hasta mañana!

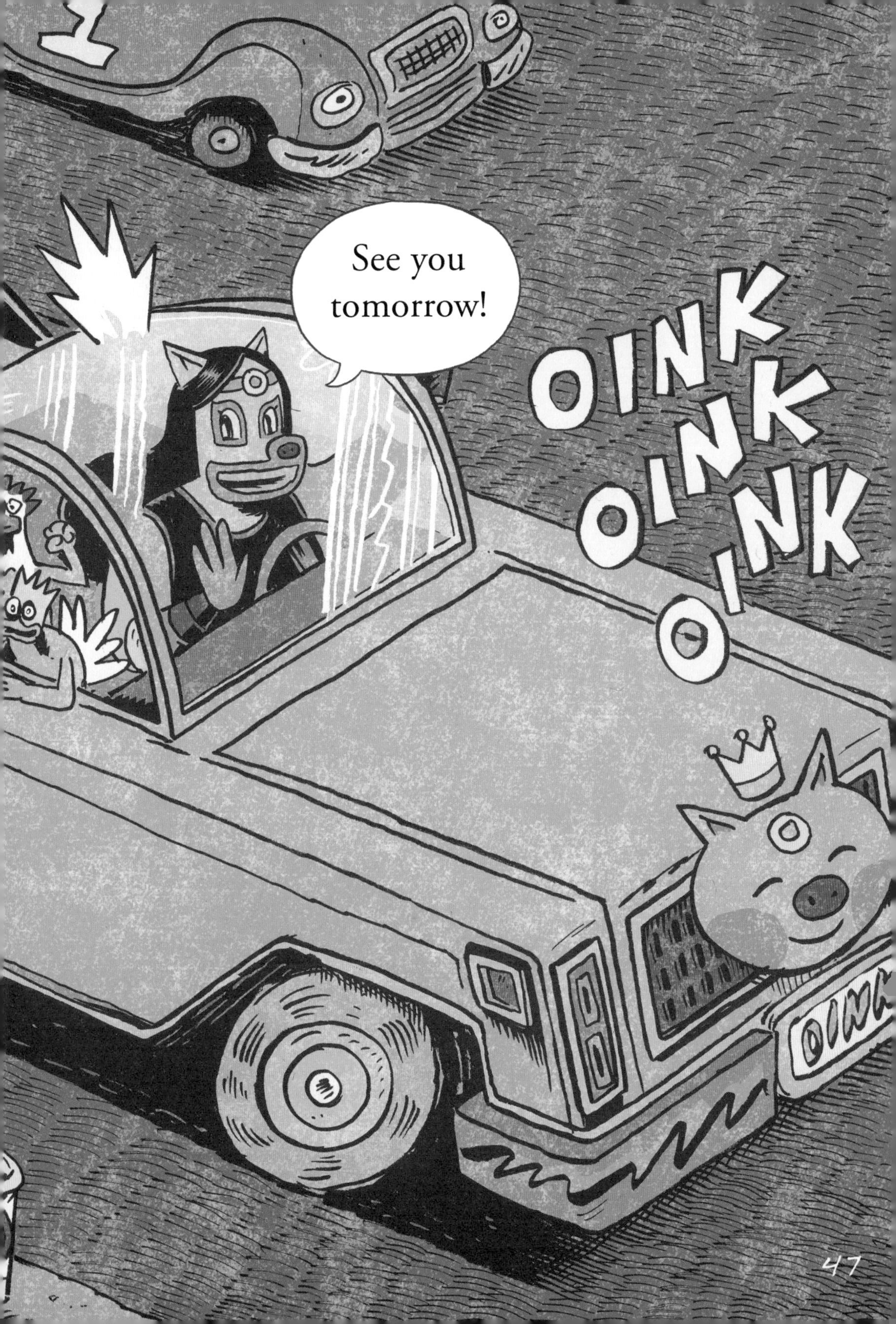
See you tomorrow!
OINK OINK OINK OINK

To my spectacular tag team partner, Elaine.
You make my drawings look so good! —Raúl the Third

To my dedicated tag team partner, Raúl the Third.
I make your drawings look spectacular! —Elaine Bay

Versify® is an imprint of Houghton Mifflin Harcourt Publishing Company.
Versify is a registered trademark of Houghton Mifflin Harcourt Publishing Company.

hmhbooks.com

The illustrations in this book were done in ink on smooth plate Bristol board with Adobe Photoshop for color.
The text type was set in Adobe Garamond LT Std.
Hand lettering by Raúl Gonzalez III
Design by Natalie Fondriest

The Library of Congress Cataloging-in-Publication data is on file.

ISBN: 978-0-358-38039-9

Manufactured in China
SCP 10 9 8 7 6 5 4 3 2 1
4500816171

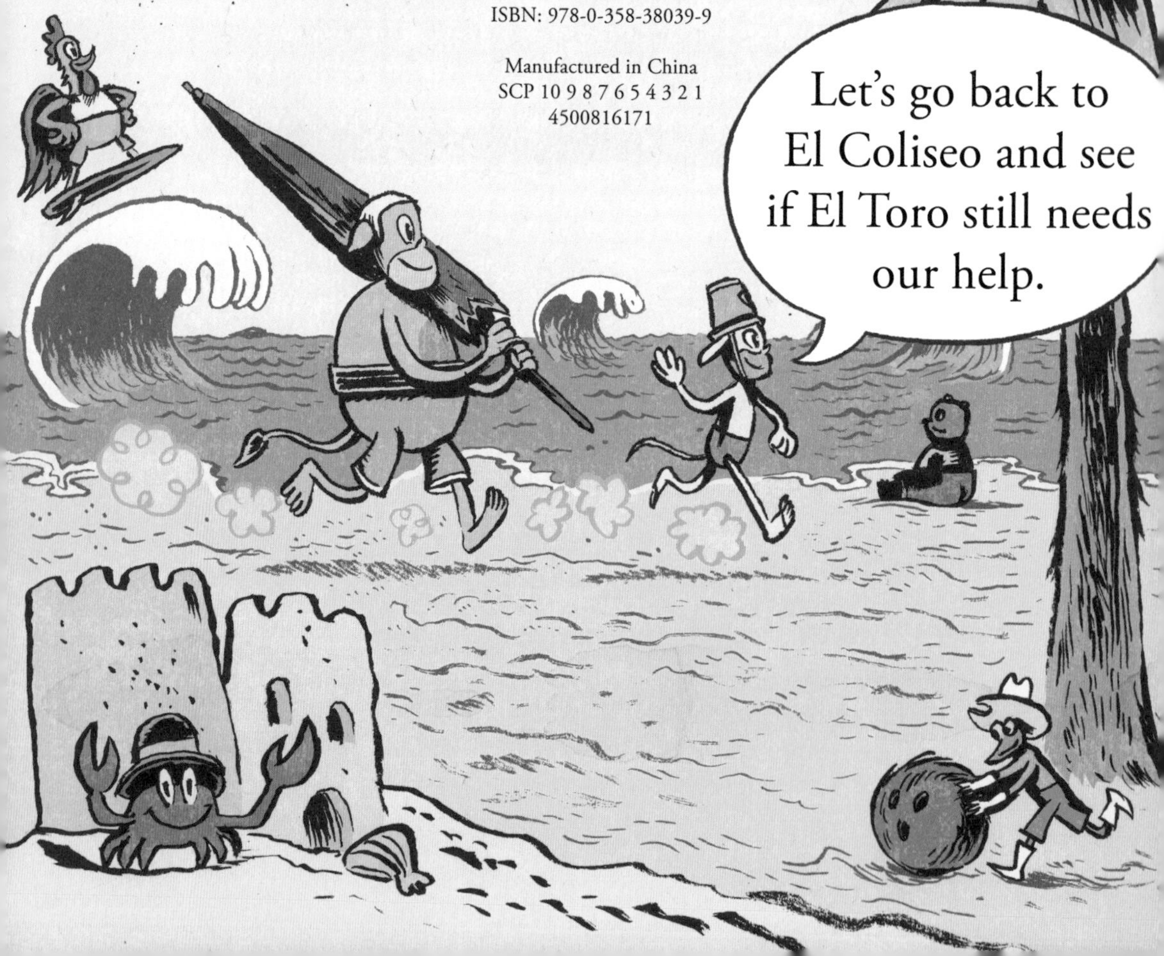
Let's go back to El Coliseo and see if El Toro still needs our help.

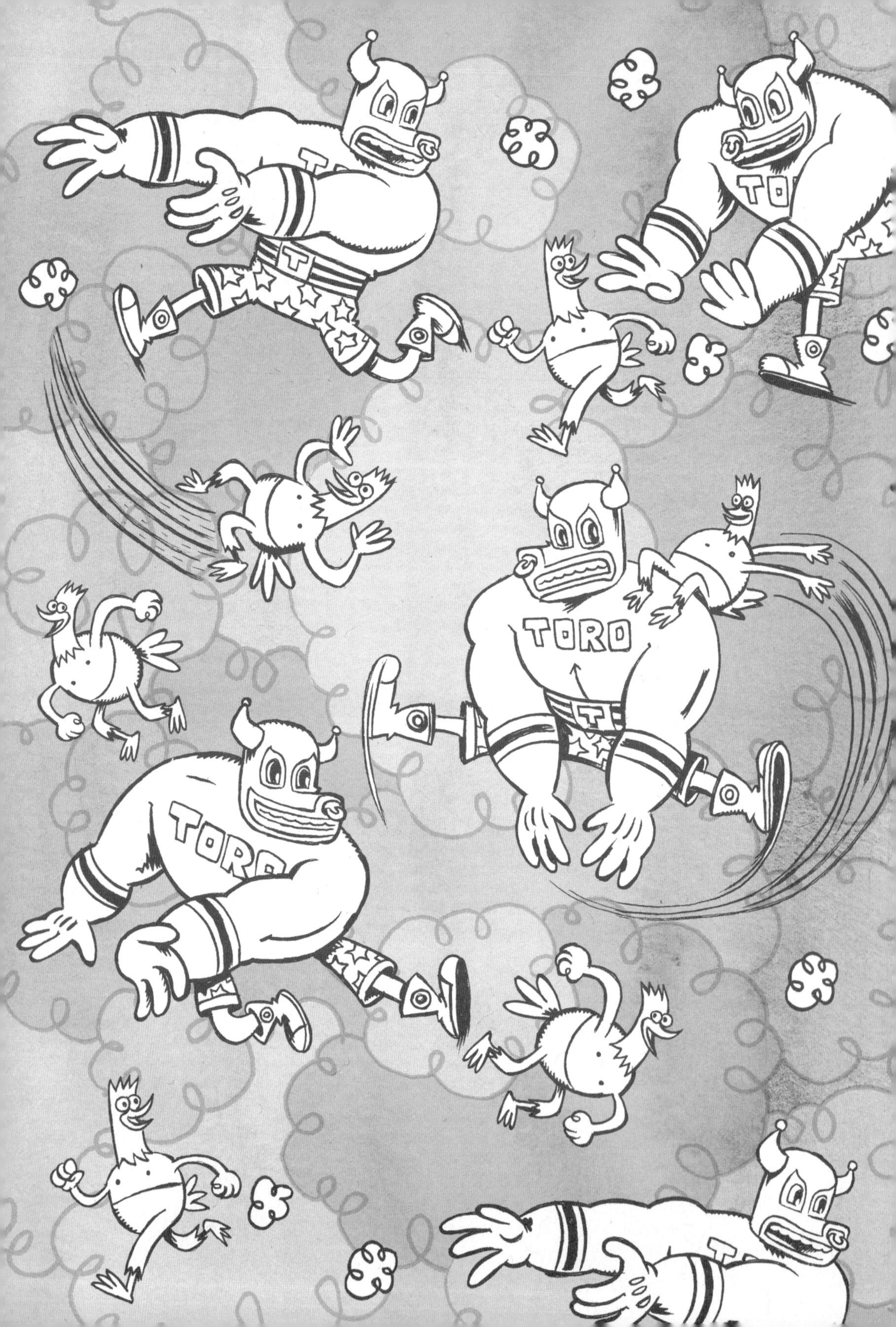
TORO
TORO
TORO
TORO